Destiny Razed

Felicia Jedlicka

Book 3

For those who believe love & faith are the same word.

More titles by FELICIA JEDLICKA

DESTINY REJECTED
DESTINY RECLAIMED
DESTINY RAZED
DESTINY RESTORED

DÉJÀ VU

SAVE THE HUMANS

THE NECROMANCER'S CHILD

SISTER WITCHES
THE DEVIL'S SHADOW
THE DEVIL'S SOUL

THE NEBRASKA APOCALYPSE NOVELS
CORN COWS AND THE APOCALYPSE
COW TIPPING AFTER THE APOCALYPSE
CORN HUSKING AFTER THE APOCALYPSE

THE WARDEN SERIES
SUCCESSORS
RIVALS
LOVERS AND LIARS
BAD BLOOD
TENANTS AND TYRANTS
THE RING BEARER
GODS AND MONSTERS
BEASTS AND BURDENS
MAGIC AND MAYHEM
FORK IN THE ROAD
DETAILS AND DEADLINES

Destiny Razed

FELICIA JEDLICKA

Falling Apart

I should probably say that my life flashed before my eyes, but in a life-or-death situation, your thoughts are very definitive and at the moment. My first thoughts, of course, were, "Holy shit, I'm going to die." Most people, I imagine, would think something very similar. It's the second and third thoughts that determine whether you will die or almost die.

The gravity released just as the shuttle fragmented. I barely got my last breath before the vacuum of space ripped it away from me. I could feel the explosion of the thruster fuel hot on my back, but with the air escaping so quickly, it didn't have enough time to scorch me before it extinguished again. It was the universe's frosty grip that burned my skin.

Glass and metal shrapnel hurled past me, putting rents in my skin. I didn't bleed, though. My blood froze even before it could clot. I tried to keep my eyes open, to search for some miraculous escape route, but there were no garbage disposals to crawl into. There wasn't even a ship close enough to hammer my fists against.

It was at this moment that I thought about what I really wanted in life—or would—if I wasn't asphyxiating. To my surprise, it wasn't about the romantic notion of choosing between my love for Terrin or Rayne. It wasn't even about my truest friends, Ayil or Aresties. The only thing I could think about at that moment was that I wanted to go home. Not home to my ship, where I had lived for so many years, but home to my family. My mother, my father, and my baby sister. The place I had avoided for seven years.

The irony was not lost on me.

When I had breathed the last of my air and the crucial seconds for a potential rescue had nearly lapsed, something impacted my body. The force threw me to one side as something warm surrounded me—as if someone had thrown a blanket over me. The fabric tightened around me until it completely encased me. I heard a clicking noise and then a "whoosh" as air filled the interior of the cocoon. I took a deep breath, restoring my oxygen and sending my head into a rush of dizziness.

After a moment, I felt a tingle of electricity permeating my enclosure and I got the sense that I was being drawn in by a retraction field. It wasn't until I felt gravity restore, and my body dropped to a hard metal floor, that I knew I was safe—from space death, at least. I couldn't be sure whose ship I was on or what they would do to me.

I ripped open the bag and untwisted the endless knots and ties. Just as I crawled out of my containment into a darkened room, I saw Ayil next to me, struggling to get out of his. I squeezed my upper body out and assisted him. When we were finally free, we embraced, taking just a moment to rejoice in our continued lives.

The sweet moment quickly evaporated when whatever ship we had arrived on took fire. The floor vibrated from each impact. There was a dull echo in the room from discharges hitting the outer hull. With each quiver of the ship and resounding boom, I became more confident that the shields were holding and that we weren't about to die—again.

Ayil and I pulled ourselves up and explored the small cargo bay of the unfamiliar ship. A cursory glance had already told me that this wasn't part of the Coalition's fleet. Their ships didn't have traditional cargo bays—since they didn't carry cargo. They carried soldiers and jetships, and that was about it.

However, if we weren't on the battlerunner, where were we? There had been another ship on my screen when we arrived, but I hadn't been able to identify it. Had friends or enemies rescued us? Someone may have rescued us, but that didn't mean we were free.

The room was empty. There wasn't an ounce of equipment or even supplies for us to rummage through for weapons. There was only the bay door, an entrance door, and a tiny intercom screen beside it.

I looked at Ayil and he nodded his permission. I pressed the button to call out and waited.

And waited.

I pressed the button several more times and finally, a bald man appeared on the screen. "What?" he asked, as if we were interrupting his supper.

I shrugged. "Ah, hello."

"Yes, yes, hello. What? What do you need?"

"I need to know where I am and who you are."

"Can it wait? I'm kind of in the middle of a battle here?"

"Are you battling the Coalition?" I asked, in case that might reveal the nature of my savior.

He chuckled. "The Coalition knows better than to waste their time with me, but General Sanders is quite a determined woman."

"General Sanders?" My heart rejoiced. "The empire did send out a fleet," I said, more to Ayil than to the man on the screen.

"She is quite inventive on the battlefield," he said rather dreamily. "It's a shame that we were never properly introduced. I would have enjoyed engaging her in conversation."

"Where are we? What ship is this?"

"It's my ship," the man clarified, as if I were stupid for asking.

"No, what affiliation are you? What government do you work for?"

"No governments. I hate politics."

"Then why are you fighting the empire?"

"I have no wish to fight her. She attacked me."

"She attacked you because you have me. Sir, you need—"

"Captain," he corrected.

"Captain, you need to—"

"Captain Reynard Baloch," he specified.

"Baloch?" I looked at Ayil for confirmation that I had heard the name correctly. "Are you any relation to Rayne Baloch?"

"Yes, that's me," Reynard said.

"That's who?" I asked.

"Me. I am Captain Rayne Baloch." He looked away from the screen for a moment and shrugged. "What? She asked."

I looked at Ayil and found the same dread on his face that I felt. Something wasn't right about this. "Captain, you can stop this battle with one call. Just contact General Sanders and let her know that I am safe. Then she can send out a shuttle to retrieve us."

Reynard's face whipped back to the screen. "Oh, no, I'm afraid we are well past that point. You will not be returning to the empire or the Coalition. You will be staying right here with me."

"Are you saying I'm your prisoner?"

He winced as if he smelled something awful. "No, of course not. You are my guests."

"Guests who can't leave?" Ayil asked.

"Ugh, can we please discuss this later? The general needs my attention, and I refuse to miss a moment of her verbal tirade."

"Why won't you let us leave?" I asked.

He paused a moment. "For protection." The monitor clicked off and despite pressing the button several more times, he didn't come back.

GUESTS

Sometime later, the explosions stopped, and we settled in for a boring and worrisome wait.

I stared across the dark expanse to Ayil's draping form. He wasn't crying anymore, just hunched over from a deep morose. I couldn't blame him. They destroyed our ship. We had just shot Edric and Aresties out into space pods, not knowing where they might end up. The pods were designed to go to the nearest habitable planet on record, but then what? Would they arrive together? Who would find them? Once again, alive and safe, were not synonymous.

I couldn't imagine the worry that Ayil was feeling. Though Aresties was carrying my baby, I couldn't equate my concerns to his. In truth, after we transferred the fetus to her, my maternal instincts—such as they were—seemed to dry up. I felt so disconnected from the pregnancy that I frequently forgot I had been pregnant to begin with.

I was apparently running away from that responsibility as well.

Now Ayil and I had this strange new kidnapper to deal with. On one hand, the captain had protected us from a cold, space death, so he most likely didn't want to kill us. But on the other, he was obviously not willing to let us go. Which raised the basic question of, what does he want from me? Was he after my eggs, my money, or my bounty?

And why did he claim that capturing me was for protection? Not my protection or his protection, just protection. Whose protection? Perhaps he was acting as a third party, impartial to the political climate. Was he trying to prevent a war? If the Coalition knew my mother had retrieved me, maybe they would attack Brahama. No, that was suicide.

It was true that the Coalition had very advanced military operations. As evident by the biomechanoid army and their weapons systems. However, the Coalition was a rather small planetary union. They had less than a dozen planets under their government. Whereas my mother's empire counted the populations of over a dozen systems. She was, by only the tiniest of exaggeration, a galactic queen.

Surely, the Coalition wouldn't dare attack the home planet of an empress? Then again, they had a rather sordid history with the empire. I had assumed that my cross-planetary rearing had eased the tension between the two governments—and I suppose it had—until I left. No doubt each side was blaming the other for my loss. Yet another fault to add on my naughty list.

Regardless of why the captain had rescued me, I was naturally suspicious of anyone who wanted to help me. Especially when this helpful hand came with an even bigger question mark than usual. He was claiming to be Captain Rayne Baloch, a man that I thus far had known only as my husband, a former hitman (a lazy emphasis on former), and the father of my child.

Rayne—my Rayne—was still being contained on Miorita, the home planet of the gattaw and the location of the legendary *dogfights*. The politics behind the gladiator-style entertainment had left me with very few options to bail him out. Once the biomechanoids arrived in the arena, my opportunities to retrieve him evaporated. His sacrifice to help me save Terrin, my former childhood bodyguard, was now biting us in the ass. It was becoming more and more difficult to keep all of my friends out of harm's way at the same time.

"Ayil, I'm so sorry," I whispered across the room to Ayil.

He raised his head and looked at me. A sliver of light filtered down on his face from a crack in the floor above. I could see just a glimpse of his bloodshot brown eyes. His angular cheekbones looked blushed—irritated by his vigorous attempts to wipe away the evidence of his tears. His normally silky brown locks clung to his forehead, making him look like the teenager I had met years ago.

When we first met, Ayil latched onto me like a life preserver. He begged me to free him from captivity and I couldn't help but play his heroine. Which was insane, because I barely knew what I was doing. I had only just figured out the difficulties of my nomadic lifestyle. However, for some reason, he trusted me and devoted himself to me.

Though my love for him was decidedly familial, I wasn't blind to how stunningly attractive he was. If forced prostitution had not consumed his past—or perhaps if I had not already been in love with two unattainable men—we might have been more to each other than friends. As it stood, though, I considered our friendship to be the most reliable relationship in my life.

Despite that bond, Ayil gave me a look that made me wilt. I wasn't used to being the target of his wrath. "Why do you keep apologizing?" he asked.

"Because this is all my fault."

"What is all your fault?" he asked.

"The biomechanoids, being here on Miorita, everything that has happened to all of you from day one, has been my fault."

"And you think that we are all so cowardly that we couldn't say no to you if we wanted to?"

"No, that's not what I—"

"You think you're so powerful and influential that we wouldn't dare speak for ourselves?"

"No, of course not."

"Then we are dimwitted and ignorant and can't think for ourselves?"

"You know I don't mean any of that."

"Then stop apologizing!" he yelled. His voice reverberated off the walls. I sunk my head against my knees, feeling properly chastised for taking more than my share of the blame. After a moment, Ayil spoke softly to me. "Where do you think he is?" he asked.

I looked up and furrowed my brow at him. "They are probably already on Miorita." He didn't seem to like that idea, since Miorita was no place for humans. "I bet Aresties is already buying him some belly beans and walking him around the market."

I smiled at that thought. It was a nice thought. I didn't know where they were, or if they were even alive.

Ayil nodded readily, accepting my positive attitude, which was a pleasant change of pace for me. He continued to stare across the room at me. "How are you holding up?" he asked—now focusing his worry on me instead of himself.

I shrugged, considering my loss carefully.

Aresties had been part of my crew even longer than Ayil, and she was just as loyal to me. It was no surprise that she had volunteered to take on the role of my surrogate. It was a risk to transfer the fetus, but ultimately safer for everyone involved. Since I was being hunted for my DNA—my offspring would have been just as coveted.

When I put her in that pod, I had no expectation of seeing her again, but only because I wasn't sure I was going to make it.

"I'm sure they are all fine. Baby too."

"No," Ayil said. "I mean, Terrin."

I stared blankly at Ayil, trying to figure out what he was talking about. After a second, I realized he still thought Terrin was dead. He hadn't recognized him past his old man disguise at the arena. Genaro, Terrin's father, had taken his place in the pit. He had died to save his son and restore the family name. It was a noble sacrifice I was exceptionally grateful for.

Even as the words to assure Ayil came out of my mouth, a vibration started in the floor. We both looked down at the rumbling metal beneath us, then back at each other. A loud clunk signaled a docking ship, and we looked toward the noise. Above the outer bay door, a tiny light flashed, and a beep resonated through the room.

Someone new had arrived.

Ayil jumped to his feet and started searching the empty room for some manner of weapon. He found a long piece of shrapnel that his retrieval balloon had dragged in and he swung it to get a feel for its weight.

He approached the interior door just as it creaked and shuddered. As it lifted open, light pierced the room, blinding me. My only view through the rising door was a set of sturdy legs. The smell of stale air replaced the musty odor of the bay.

As soon as we could see the upper torso of our guest, Ayil charged him. He obviously wasn't taking any chances. Too many people had gotten the upper hand on us lately.

Unfortunately, the man saw him coming and wrenched the shrapnel axe away from him. When Ayil tried a more physical attack, the man just pushed him to the floor and pushed his foot on his chest to hold him down.

"Ayil, stop," he bellowed.

"Holy shit," Ayil whispered. "Terrin?"

I was still blinking against the light, unable to recognize the man before me until the silhouette of his horns came into view. Relief melted the tension from my muscles. "Terrin."

His head snapped up, eyes looking at me like I was his prey. I moved forward a little, resisting the temptation to barrel him over with a hug until I was certain he recognized me. After a moment to examine me, he beckoned me over. I moved to him and he instigated the embrace. "Mallory," he whispered in my ear. "I heard your ship had been destroyed."

"Aresties and Edric were sent out in the escape pods," I mumbled into his chest. "How did you get aboard?" I looked up, ready to hear about any potential rescue plots he might have. Instead, he swooped down and kissed me.

It was not our usual greeting. And the sweet thank-god-you're-alive-kiss was far more intimate than friends should share. When his tongue probed to tickle mine, I nearly pushed him off from the shock. Nearly, but not quite. Instead, my knees gave out, and I found my only stability was what he provided by his bracing arms. I felt a warmth spread over me as temptation licked its way from my lips down to my belly.

For a moment, I was back in the grips of my fifteen-year-old crush again. Drawn in by the exotic nature of a male gattaw. A common problem for me to be sure, but usually Terrin didn't encourage my naïve notion of a carnal union. Since we were biologically incompatible, there was no happily ever after in store for us.

Not without a great deal of pain.

Terrin showed no sign of letting up his kiss and, since I was just a hapless victim, I played my part far better than a married woman should. It wasn't until Ayil—who was still being crushed under Terrin's boot—interrupted us that I came to my senses.

"Excuse me!" Ayil grumbled.

I drew away from Terrin, but he didn't seem willing to let me go just yet. The carnivorous look in his eyes had not waned, making the ardor pooling in my stomach sink lower.

"I thought you were dead," Ayil added.

"Ayil, I'm so sorry. I didn't get a chance to tell you." Ayil shifted his perturbed look at me.

"My father took my place in the pit," Terrin explained.

Ayil shifted his attention back to Terrin. His eyes flickered over his face, which still bore a few flakes of his elderly disguise. As he fully gleaned the sacrifice that had taken place, his eyes softened. "I'm sorry. Your father was a good man."

"Thank you." Terrin released me and helped Ayil off the floor. He placed a firm grip on the young man's shoulder and squeezed it. "A word of advice. Don't try to attack a man fresh out of the dogfights. If I hadn't recognized you, I might have snapped your neck."

"Are you sure you aren't still trying?" Ayil squirmed under his grip.

Terrin gave him a small smirk and released his shoulder. He looked around the empty bay before turning to me. He noticed the blood trickling down my arm and moved to inspect what turned out to be a rather deep cut in my right bicep. "I have a first aid kit in my shuttle." Terrin ducked back into his shuttle and popped back out with the kit.

"Is that thing parked or locked in?" Ayil asked, eyeballing his transportation.

"Locked in, why?" He moved to me and pulled my arm forward to tend to my injury. His tenderness, as he dabbed the antiseptic on my cut, didn't surprise me. Terrin had always been more reserved than his brethren, urbane even. However, his warning to Ayil was justified. Not more than a day earlier, he had been competing in the dogfights, savagely beating his opponents into a bloody mess. "What's going on?"

"We're stuck here," Ayil said. "That's what's going on."

"Hasn't he let you in?" Terrin asked as he placed a bandage over my cut.

"No, he..." I furrowed my brow and exchanged a glance with Ayil. "How did you even know we were on this ship? Did he contact you?"

"Yes, Rayne filled me in on the basics and instructed me to dock here."

"So you've met our new friend, Captain Rayne?" I said sarcastically.

"What do you mean, I've met him?" Terrin asked. "Of course, I've met Rayne."

"Wait a minute. You spoke with our Rayne?" I asked. "He contacted you? From this ship? He's not on Miorita?"

Terrin glanced at Ayil, no doubt to see if I had suddenly gone insane, but Ayil had the same concerned look on his face. "Who have you been communicating with?"

"Yoo-hoo." The high-pitched call carried over from the communication screen by the entrance door. "That would be me." We all approached the monitor, each of us with expressions of irritation, curiosity, and downright murderous intent in Ayil's case. "I'm so sorry for the confusion. I wasn't sure that you would be comfortable docking on the ship of a complete stranger."

"Who are you?" Terrin asked.

"Oh heavens, they haven't introduced me yet? I am Captain Rayne Baloch."

"It just so happens that we have a friend with that same name," Terrin said diplomatically. "Is it possible that you are merely masquerading under a false name?"

The balding man twisted his features as if to consider this question. "Technically, yes, but to be fair, Reynard really is a tough name for a child to grow up with. You wouldn't believe how many times I've been called Reynard, the retard. Which is completely ridiculous, since I am a veritable genius."

"Are you saying—" Terrin began.

"I'm not just saying that either. I've taken tests. Look at the technology I've created. Do you know how many people have tried to buy me out? Or better yet, how many people have tried to kill me and take my technology?" Reynard leaned into the camera, making his face even larger on the screen. "Let's put it this way, you and me, Princess. We could share horror stories."

"Does that mean—" Terrin once again tried to interject.

"Oh, don't get me wrong, it's given me the inspiration to invent some of my most creative works. One of which you've used, my dear. That shield you have pinned to your chin." He motioned to his own chin. I instinctively reached for the tiny button that was taped beneath my chin. A shield, but also a disguise. It was off now, but it had been integral to my escape from Miorita.

"The weaponry that I've created might be as much glitz and glam as anything, but it's the little things that have established my brilliance and made me indispensable to my clientele." Reynard looked at someone off-screen and grimaced. "Yes, yes." He looked back at the camera. "Apparently I'm dragging on. How can I not when the subject is me?" The man laughed and snorted at his own joke. "Let's get down to business, shall we?"

"Yes, let's," Terrin grumbled.

"Let me start by saying how delighted I am to have you here, Your Highness. I've heard so much about you. It's a shame we haven't met before this, but I have been watching you for quite some time."

"How creepy," I said with false cheer.

"Since birth, really," he added.

"And it just got creepier," Ayil said.

"Let me guess, you want to harvest a dozen of my best eggs?"

"No, not at all," the captain immediately rejected the idea as if it was a despicable thought to him. "Your DNA, while invaluable, is much too dangerous to be played with, like currency."

"Then why are we here?" Ayil asked.

Captain Reynard looked off screen for a moment and shrugged at whoever was talking to him. "My hope is to contain your DNA, not spread it."

"And who made it your job to contain my DNA?"

Reynard's face turned sour, and he glared right back at me. "You really don't know who I am, do you?"

"Should I?"

"Yes, but no. Anonymity is best for a man like me. However, it would be much easier if you understood how many wars have been thwarted because of me? Singular acts, like moves on a chessboard. I can dismantle armies, annihilate threats, and extinguish the desire for vengeance."

"Are you saying you're one of the good guys?" I asked.

Reynard hissed between his front teeth. "That's a feminine ideal. White knights that don't get stained with blood. I don't claim to be the hero. I just make sure that the wars that deserve to be fought are fought fairly."

"You're a weapon designer?" Terrin asked.

"Yes, and a very good one."

"Who do you work for?" he asked.

"No one, I'm self-employed."

"You must have worked for someone. You said you've been watching Mallory since birth. Since she spent her childhood on two planets and under close supervision, I must surmise that you are a former employee of one of those governments."

Reynard's mouth hung open for a moment before he laughed. He poked his finger at the screen. "Oh, you are good. Not the buffoon that your species is credited for. I was told not to underestimate you."

"And who told you that?" Terrin asked.

Reynard answered, but the ship rocked with a tremor. "Oh, for the love of... She found us already. Hasn't that woman got an ounce of indolence? I'm afraid we'll have to talk later."

"Captain, I demand that you let us out immediately and allow us to rendezvous with the general," I spouted defiantly.

"No," Reynard said flatly.

"Then we will break out of here and continue this discussion on the bridge while Terrin throttles you."

Reynard paused a moment before sputtering into laughter. "Didn't I mention that I'm a weapons designer? My entire ship is booby-trapped. You are welcome to test the systems, but I would strongly recommend that you wait so I can properly adjust the parameters to your presence."

"I'm done with these games. I want out of here."

Reynard's face instantly darkened. "Have it your way then, but leaving that bay means that the games are just beginning." He smiled broadly, bearing perfectly white, but crooked teeth. "Good luck."

The communication screen shut off and, as promised, the door to the cargo bay opened. I was happy to be free of my darkened containment until the pulse blasts started.

BLINƌ

Pulse blasts came through the door the moment it opened. Ayil dove left, I dove right, and Terrin leaped deeper into the cargo bay. Each of us cussed and grumbled as we did.

"Seriously, who the hell is this guy?" Ayil asked after the firing had subsided.

"I think it's a toss-up between evil genius and mad scientist," I said.

"Either way, it makes us rats in his maze," Terrin said. "Perhaps we should consider waiting here, as he advised." Despite his suggestion, he inched forward and drew his copper sword.

"If Sanders is keeping him busy, this might be our only chance to get the upper hand," I argued. "He's a techno-geek, so he probably doesn't even have that many guards. We just need to make it past his weapons and we can get the drop on him."

Terrin nodded and waved his sword across his path as he neared the door again. Another barrage of pulses demanded his retreat. "It's motion-sensor activated."

"I don't suppose you brought a pulse pistol with you so we can just blast the damn thing?" I asked.

"Sadly, no," Terrin said.

"What about re-breathers?" I asked.

Terrin's brow dipped. "Only two."

"Grab them, then bring me your sword."

Terrin slipped back into his shuttle and returned a moment later with two small air filtration masks. They weren't the best for long-term use, but they worked for multiple situations, including oxygen deprivation situations. Which, depending on your ship, could be a normal occurrence.

Terrin tossed one mask to Ayil and, after carefully avoiding the weapons' line of sight, brought the other to me. He glanced at his sword somewhat longingly before handing it to me.

I used it to pry open the electrical panel containing the communications screen. Behind the panel were various wires and cords. "Ayil, take your shirt off."

Ayil looked down at his shirt, then at Terrin. "Can't you just use his?"

I glanced at Terrin. He rolled his eyes before shrugging out of his tunic and handing it to me. His broad shoulders still bore the marks of his months of gladiator-style combat on *Miorita*. It was a grueling and relentless abuse to his body, but I also knew that some of his bruises were from the ladies that visited him between the fights. A perk of the winner's circle.

I ignored the stab of jealousy I felt for his other lovers and the guilt that followed that unnecessary emotion—since I wasn't his lover in any sense of the word. That was, of course, yet another issue that would need to be dealt with later. An awkward conversation to redefine the boundaries of our friendship after making out with him in his cell—and the impromptu snogging five minutes ago.

I yanked out a few wires until I found the electrical line. Holding the cloth up to the live line, I watched the material blacken and form a flame. I gingerly set down the cloth as the flame took hold. The tiny pile smoked, filling the enclosed space with enough haze to set off the fire alarm. The familiar urgent chirping demanded that we exit the area immediately or suffer a lung-clogging mist.

Terrin reached around me, pressing the mask onto my face just as the alarm let out a final bleat and a yellowish powder plumed from tiny ducts in the ceiling and walls. Terrin yelled behind me and shifted suddenly. I looked back and found him rubbing his tearing eyes. The spray of fire retardant smeared yellow across his face. "Terrin?"

"Go!" He waved me on.

Besides smothering out the fire with a nonflammable layer of silt and making the air inhospitable to breathe, it created a smog that disguised our presence to the motion-activated weaponry just outside the door.

Practically blinded by my plan of escape, Terrin grabbed my shoulder and allowed me to lead him from the room. With little more visibility than a foot in front of my face, I felt my way down the long hallway. I took a few deep breaths before handing the re-breather back to Terrin for his turn. He took a necessary inhalation and shoved it right back to me.

When we cleared the fog, we found ourselves back in front of another door. I removed my mask and turned to check Terrin's eyes, which were closed and profusely tearing up. Considering that my own eyes were stinging from the proximity to the particulate, I could only imagine what he was feeling. I stuffed my re-breather into my back pocket and reached to tend to him, but he pulled his head back. "Let me check," I insisted.

He grabbed my hands and pressed them together. "There is nothing to check. It will clear up eventually."

The communications screen flickered to life beside the door, and Reynard appeared. "You are clever. I'll give you that."

"I'm so glad to have entertained you. Now let us go."

"Not a chance. You chose to be impatient, and Terrin is suffering for it. He's lying, by the way. That shit will eat his corneas away if he doesn't get to an eye wash soon. There is one in my lab, but I'm afraid I have several booby traps between here and there."

Ayil shoved me out of the way and put his face in front of the screen. "Listen, you overgrown child. The longer you keep us jumping through hoops, the more time I have to plot the specifics of your death. So, either you let us through or I will personally feed you your own testicles."

Reynard frowned. "I'm afraid I'm not as good at angry banter as some men. I never had a knack for extemporaneous threats. However, what I do have a knack for is defending myself, so I would very much like to see you try to accomplish the task that you have illustrated. And you'll get your chance as soon as you can get to me."

"Why don't you come down here and fight me yourself, Reynard the retard?"

Reynard's lips pursed, and his face turned red. His face crumpled as if he might cry, but then darkness bled into his expression again. "I don't like that turn of phrase," he said simply. Before any of us could react to the shifting panel

below the communications screen, a muzzle emerged, and
a shot fired.

Leash

I screamed and shoved Ayil aside, but I was much too late. We both landed in a heap on the floor. Ayil groaned in pain as I frantically searched him for injury. I found a trace of blood and a metal point poking through a hole in his shirt. I ripped open the cloth to see the extent of the wound, but the smattering of blood on the cloth was the bulk of it. Instead of a hole in his chest, a tiny device had unfurled, clamping its metal talons into his skin like a toothy leech.

"What the hell is that?" Ayil strained his neck to see the metal spider web connected to him. He reached for it and yanked, but he yelped and withdrew his hand. "Bugger zapped me."

"I wouldn't advise removing it manually," Reynard said over the com.

"What is that thing?" Terrin asked, keeping his distance from the door.

"It's a dog leash."

"Excuse me?" I turned back to the screen to see if this was Reynard's idea of a joke.

"Well, technically, it's designed for a particular breed of dog, but its original purpose was to maintain the animal's proximity to his owner."

"So what, he can't leave this ship?" I asked.

"No, the device punishes an accelerated heart rate."

"Punishes?" Terrin asked.

"It was designed to give an electrical surge if the animal reaches a running pace. It keeps them slow enough for their owner to keep up with them."

"If Ayil's heart rate exceeds a certain level, it will give him a zap." Reynard grimaced and looked away from the screen. "What? He insulted me."

"Reynard." I approached the screen, despite Terrin tugging on my shoulder. "What exactly happens if Ayil's heart rate exceeds the specified parameters?"

"He'll get a warning shock that will incapacitate him, but if his heart rate doesn't come down within a minute, he'll get the full shock."

"Which will do what?"

"The device was designed for an eight-hundred-pound creature."

"What will it do!" I yelled at the screen.

"His heart will stop."

I froze and stared at the screen for a moment. Ayil had calmed considerably, taking in slow breaths to slow his heart rate. "I assume extracting it will produce a similar result."

"Yes."

"You son of a bitch! I hope Sanders shoots you on sight."

Reynard twisted his lips as he glared at me. "I wish you knew who I was. This would be a lot easier."

"Why, so I can fear you?"

"No, so you can show me some respect."

The compartment below the monitor opened again, and another muzzle came out. There was a swoosh sound before the tiny barrel shot a needle-headed dart into my leg. I grabbed the end and immediately ripped it out. I felt the tip tug against my skin as if the head had a barbed end. Although it wasn't a pleasant experience, I knew better than to assume the pain was the worst of the weapon's offense. "What did you just do to me?"

"I'm slowing you down, too. Now you each have a handicap. Terrin must trust his safety to another's eyes. Ayil must restrict his reactions, even while under extreme duress. And as soon as your total-body paralysis sets in, you'll only have your brain to get you out of this mess." Reynard leaned forward, enlarging his image on the screen. "I do so hope you're enjoying yourself, Princess, because you've got a long way to go before you get to me."

WEIGHT

errin yanked me away from the monitor to keep me from bruising my fists any further. "Mallory, stop."

"I am going to kill that asshole!"

"Not if I get to him first!" Ayil gripped the door, trying to spread it open. He growled when his brute strength only shifted the door slightly before closing up tight again.

"Both of you settle down. We aren't going to do anything until we get to him. Mallory, what's happening to you?"

"I can feel a tingling in my legs, but I can walk still."

"Good. Ayil, you need to keep your movements to a minimum."

"What, I just stand around while you two save the day?"

Terrin moved closer to him. His eyes were open, but I could tell from his vacant gaze and bloodshot eyes that he was still blind. "Ayil, this isn't a life-or-death situation. We can simply stop here and wait for Reynard to come fetch us."

"No, we can't," I said. "We have to get you to an eye wash now, remember? We have to keep going."

As if on cue, the door to the next section slid open. Ayil and I jumped back. Terrin followed suit, when Ayil tugged on his arm. Ayil waved his hand across the entrance, but nothing shot it off. He peeked around, giving the area a quick survey before tucking back in. "There's nothing there."

I peeked around and checked the hall. The slight curvature of the ship was enough to keep the next door out of view, but I hoped it wouldn't be too far away. "I don't get it. What's the catch?" I took a step forward and felt my leg give out. I tried to recover, but the other gave out and I dropped to the floor. "Shit," I whispered.

"Mallory?" Terrin approached my position.

"I think I'm going to need a little help to get up. I can't feel my feet."

Terrin reached down and wrapped his arm around me. After a boost to my feet, I realized that walking was also going to be an issue, so I kept my hand firmly latched to his shoulder. Ayil took the lead, allowing Terrin to rest his free hand on his shoulder.

Our first few steps were apprehensive since we were naturally expecting more weapon fire. However, nothing popped out of the walls to shoot us or trap us.

"What's the deal?" Ayil asked ahead of us. "Nothing is stopping us."

"Keep watching," Terrin instructed. "Yell, if I need to duck."

"Don't worry, I'll be screaming if a spider drops from the ceiling."

"I can see the door," Ayil panted.

"Ayil, your breathing has increased," Terrin said. "What are you doing?"

"Nothing, I'm just walking. But the air does seem a little thin."

"I feel it too," I said as I slid my feet across the floor, shuffling beside Terrin. After a few more steps, the pressure denying my feet a smooth movement transferred to the rest of my leg muscles. "It's the gravity."

"It feels like it's increasing with every step," Ayil complained.

I examined the floor grids, which were different in this section. "I don't know how he did it, but he's made some kind of gravitational quicksand."

"Ahh!" Ayil yelled. The shock from his electrical surge snapped at the end of my fingertips.

"Ayil, you must slow your movements." Terrin scolded.

"You think!"

Terrin shifted his hand to Ayil's neck, checking his pulse. I mentally counted in my head.

Four.

"Slow breaths," Terrin insisted.

"I'm trying."

"Long breath in and hold."

"I know how to breathe," Ayil snapped.

Ten.

"This isn't a joke," Terrin said.

"Do I sound like I am laughing?"

"Ayil, please," I begged.

Fifteen.

"Focus!" Terrin yelled.

"I can't focus with you yelling at me!"

"Terrin," I whispered, not wanting to alarm Ayil anymore than he already was.

Twenty.

Terrin released me and I flopped to the floor, piling on my spaghetti legs. He reached around Ayil, placing his neck in the crook of his elbow. Ayil naturally struggled. "Trust me, Ayil," Terrin whispered into his ear. Ayil gripped his arm, and despite the suffocating appearance of the hold, he was still breathing.

Twenty-five.

Ayil's hands went limp and his body slumped against Terrin. He eased him to the floor and released his grip.

Thirty.

I breathed a sigh of relief and crawled across the floor on my hands and knees. I was effectively dragging my calves and feet, but that was better than weighing down Terrin anymore than necessary. "I'll race you," I joked and glanced back at Terrin.

"Slow and steady." He winked, and I laughed.

"Wait, which one of us is the turtle in this scenario?" I asked.

"Is that yet another crack about the color of my skin? Seems a little demeaning."

"Not at all. Frog to tortoise. That's gotta be an upward move, doesn't it?" I grunted, straining against the new gravitational pull undermining my progress.

Terrin chuckled.

"How can you two be flirting at a time like this?" Ayil asked as he struggled to rise again.

"That's strange. I thought I was smack-talking," I grunted, barely able to push my arms forward. "Hey, this gravity-feed doesn't make sense."

"How's that?" Ayil took a small step forward, then rested before taking the next step.

"I mean, we aren't being pulled to the floor as much as pushed away from that end of the hallway. He's got to be using two different feeds."

"Hey, Kit, how about you just assume that we have no idea what you are talking about and just get to the part where you tell us what to do."

"He's got to have a vertical gravity panel at the end of the hall."

"That didn't help," Ayil grumbled.

"How is the gravity pushing us away?" Terrin asked. "Wouldn't it be pulling us toward it?"

"Yeah," Ayil agreed.

"He's reversed the polarity. Instead of pulling matter toward it, it's pushing it away. Like magnets repelling."

"What do we do?" Ayil asked.

"Shut off the panels."

"Can we make it to the end?" Terrin asked.

I frowned and looked back at Ayil, who was still panting. Meanwhile, I was already carrying the weight of my lower half. "Ayil and I can't, but you might."

Terrin nodded and continued on his journey. He barely showed signs of resistance until he reached me. Then his foot rose a little slower. I reached over, pushing his heel forward, though it did little good. I scooted along next to him, but eventually, the sheer weight pressing on me was hurting my head too much to continue.

Ten feet further, Terrin fell to his knees. "The strength of it increases exponentially." He panted. "I feel like an ocean is pressing against me. How much further is it?"

I wanted to lie to him and say three feet, but I knew he would give himself a stroke if he didn't pace himself. "Seven more feet," I said.

I could see Terrin's mouth perched open as he breathed heavily—an alternative to sweating for his race. He hunkered down once again and got to his feet. Like trudging through deep mud and heavy snowdrifts at the same time, he made it three more feet.

Though it likely felt like sitting at the bottom of the ocean, Terrin leaned against the gravitational force and pushed into it as if he were pushing a heavy rock up a hill. All at once, the pressure against him released. He stumbled the last three feet and landed against the door. He slid down to the floor, taking in big gulps of air. "Now what?" he asked.

"Use your sword to pry up the panels adjacent to the door."

Terrin mumbled something as he pulled his sword out again to use it for a non-battle-worthy purpose. He jammed it into the panel joint and it popped open like a swinging door. I could see him probing the innards, debating which buttons to push or dials to twist, but in the end, he just reached in and yanked until something sparked.

I heard Ayil shriek, and a moment later, he slid past me, falling toward his destination. He let out a solemn, elongated cuss word before he crashed into the panel Terrin was working on. Ayil groaned and rolled toward Terrin, in his pocket of normal gravity, in front of the door.

Terrin did the same with the other panel, but he got it to shut off instead of reversing its reversal. I shifted to begin my crawl again, but my legs were no longer taking part in my movement. Terrin came back down the hall and scooped me up.

"Come on, rabbit, no more napping." I smiled at his humor, but I could see how exhausted he was from his climb. Carrying me would be a burden he didn't need right now.

It didn't take long for the communication screen to pop back on and Reynard's simpering smile to appear. "That looked exhausting. But it's definitely good to know that my gravity wall will not keep gattaw off my ship. However, that being said, I don't know many gattaw that are interested in my technology."

"The gattaw have no use for fancy defense systems. We fight honorably—face to face. We do not hide behind gadgets."

"Good, then it should be sufficient. Speaking of honorable, very impressive knockout hold on your friend. I was getting pretty worried there for a second. To be honest, I think I acted a little too rashly when I used that device. I just really don't like that name."

"I assure you, Reynard, no one thinks of you in that way." Terrin glanced at Ayil, but there was no hope for an apology there. Not while he was still wearing the evidence of his bullying backlash.

"You are much different from the gattaw I usually meet. A little more refined, I would say. Definitely well-spoken by comparison. And I appreciate the sincerity of your civility. I can see that you understand the value of diplomacy when dealing with an opponent."

A tremor rolled through the ship again, and Reynard yelled through his teeth. "Will one of you please shoot something critical on her! I'm tired of being nice." The screen went blank again.

Leap

The door opened to the new section. Ayil moved in first, surveying the area carefully before continuing. Terrin carried me through and we each observed the walls as carefully as we could. Much like the last section, there was a slight curve keeping the distance to the door a mystery until we rounded the bend.

It wasn't until we had nearly reached it that we saw the offensive tactic employed for this branch of our journey. The floor of the hallway stopped several yards from the door. It was a rather old-school defense following the tradition of castle moats. However, since there was only a veiled force field between us and the exterior of the ship, I knew that falling was not an option.

The field was just enough to keep the vacuum of space from sucking all the air out, but something heavy was bound to pop it like a balloon. Whomever fell through would be sucked out into space, right along with their compatriots.

"How bad is it?" Terrin asked.

"It's got to be at least fifteen feet across, but there's a pretty good ledge on the other side with the door. With a running start, I could clear it," Ayil said.

"You'd have to slow your heart rate down the second you landed." Terrin leveled a stern glare in his direction.

"I can do it," Ayil assured him. "What about you? Can you make fifteen feet with her on your back and blind?"

I could see Terrin considering the situation. His muscles shifted in his arms as if he was calculating the extra weight. My arms were still functional, but I could feel the paralysis setting into my abdomen, so I would soon only be dead weight.

"I could throw her across. You could catch her?"

"I don't know. That's pretty far to throw, especially when you can't see what you're aiming for. Maybe the force field is reinforced and we won't fall through, but we should assume that it isn't."

"What are you suggesting?" Terrin asked.

"I vote we throw her over like a sack of flour. We'll get better lift and a better chance for distance."

"There won't be anyone there to catch her if we don't make it." Terrin pointed out.

"You want to weigh in on this, Kit?"

I glanced between them and debated my options. Neither one appealed to me, but I certainly preferred the idea of someone being around to catch me. However, I could see Ayil's point. A blind man throwing a heavy object was not exactly a comforting scenario, with or without an umpire in place. "Sack of flour, it is."

After a little preparation, I lay between the two men, my arms toward Terrin and my legs near Ayil. "Now remember, Kit, you have to stay limp. Don't try to help or it might throw us off."

"This is like the worst trust exercise ever," I grumbled.

Terrin grabbed my arms, pinching them tightly, almost painfully, but I didn't complain. Whatever he needed to do to get the job done, I would endure. Ayil did the same, getting the best grip on my ankles he could. I closed my eyes, unable to think about anything other than the cold of space beneath me.

I swung, and the men counted down from five. When they reached one, they released, and I flew.

It was a short-lived flight, followed by a crash landing on the floor. Unfortunately, I landed crooked. My upper body had landed precariously close to the ledge, but since my lower body was completely useless, I couldn't straighten myself out properly. So even with three-quarters of me safe and sound, it was the quarter that was dragging me down.

My fingers slid across the floor, digging into any crevice I could get some retention from. All the while, my shoulders slipped further over the edge and my abdomen was almost useless to stop it. "Guys!"

"Kit, I'm coming over. Just hang on," Ayil yelled to me.

"Easy for you to say," I mumbled to myself, just as my clawed fingers snagged on an indentation. I held myself there, literally holding on by my fingernails.

I heard Ayil's running footsteps and a grunt as he leaped across the expanse. He landed beside me, disrupting my tenuous grip even as he grappled to maintain his own position with his upper body flopped on the ledge and his lower body scrambling to join it. I gasped and fell backward as my stomach muscles weakened and failed me. My body slipped over the ledge like a sloppy egg.

"Nope." Ayil reached over and lifted me under my back. "You're not getting away that easy." I grabbed for the floor again and between the two of us, we got my body folded in the right direction.

Ayil finished his own climb and immediately slowed his breathing before his leash tried to electrocute him again. Across the way, Terrin probed the edge of the hallway moat with his foot. He counted steps away and then returned recounting again. I could see his disappointment grow as his inconsistency caused him to arrive too late or too soon.

"You're going to have to trust us, Terrin," I called over to him.

He glanced up and nodded, but the look on his face told me it wasn't that simple. Being without his senses was as close to torture as he had likely ever been. And considering he had just left the dogfights, that was saying a lot.

Ayil started knocking on the floor next to him. The rhythmic tap seemed to help Terrin focus on his target. His next three attempts to plot steps succeeded.

He backed away, reversing his steps. As he came forward for his official attempt, Ayil guided him along. "Get ready," he yelled, "and... jump!"

Terrin leaped forward toward us. He easily cleared the expanse and crashed into the door. Unfortunately, the impact was enough to bounce him off. His arms flailed as he paddled against his unintentional ricochet. He reached the edge and nearly toppled over, but Ayil grabbed his arm and yanked him back. For a moment, Terrin gripped Ayil's arm like a life preserver. Ayil smiled at his unspoken gratitude and patted his shoulder.

"Well, well, aren't you all just team players?" Reynard's voice came over the communication screen. "I can't say I'm surprised you made it through that one. It's mostly designed to weed out heavy machinery and excessive artillery."

"Reynard, enough!" I yelled up to the screen from the floor.

"You're welcome to stop there, but by my estimation, Terrin only has about thirty minutes before that fire retardant starts to permanently frost his corneas. Tick. Tock." The screen flickered off.

Cheater

"You have got to be kidding me," Ayil grumbled beneath me.

I had taken to sitting on Terrin's shoulders to get to the ventilation shaft above us. The next challenge seemed to involve a set of heavy doors. I already suspected that it would take a very sophisticated set of codes to open them. Unfortunately, I wasn't as good at hacking as I would have preferred. My only option was to cheat.

"What is it with you and my wardrobe, woman?" Ayil shrugged out of his shirt and threw it up at me. "Do you think that I buy nice clothes just so you can destroy them?"

I glanced down and cleared my throat. Ayil stared back at me. His eyes rolled before the words reached his lips.

"No," he said resolutely. "These are Karoobian silk. They are stain proof, anti-static, and nearly impossible to find. Even on Karoo!"

"Ayil!"

"No, take his," Ayil said, once again throwing Terrin under the bus.

"Gladly," Terrin said. "But I am not wearing an undergarment. I would hate for Mallory's brainstorming to be irretrievably distracted by my glorious physique."

I snorted and flicked one of his horns.

"Oh, son of a bitch!" Ayil squawked as he shoved his pants to the floor. I caught sight of tight red spandex usually reserved for women's underwear before his pants slapped me in the face.

I threw the clothing up into the vent above me. After a great deal of help from Terrin and Ayil, I got myself into the rigid tube. Since the ship's formation was ultimately circular, all the air shafts would eventually lead to the center of the ship. And at the center of the ship, would be the most basic and important functions of space travel.

Oxygen production.

With only my upper body to drag my body through the ductwork, my movement was slow. The constant force of the air against me felt like a gale-force wind. My eyes watered, and my hands felt numb, either from the cold or the paralysis—I wasn't sure which.

I pushed onward until the duct expanded and opened out into the equivalent of a vertical jet turbine. The noise from the huge gears and rotors was minimal, even for a modern ship, but the spinning blades below and above me still offered a repetitive whoosh as it chopped through the air.

I tossed Ayil's pants down into the path of the fan blades below. The fabric immediately caught in the blades and let out a sacrificial rip before holding the turbine in stasis.

I threw his shirt toward the top fan, but the wind forced it back down again. I balled it up and tossed it into the flow, but the wind whipped it away and out of my reach.

Cussing, I removed my shirt. The effort of extracting myself from my clothing in such a tight space was enough to make me want to give up on the ridiculous endeavor altogether, but I knew unless we got the upper hand, Reynard wasn't likely to give in to any of our demands.

I pulled myself forward and reached for the cloth as high as I could. I was still too far away.

Just to my right was a utility ladder. I debated my upper body strength, but gave it a try. I kept my feet inside the tube but pulled my upper body up to give myself the extra height I needed.

Extending my reach, I pushed my shirt up against the force of the wind and into the path of the spinning blades. I cringed as I neared them, fearing my fingers might just as easily be what would jam the system.

The fabric caught and jerked away from me. My feet pulled loose and my legs dropped. The added weight was too much for me to carry and I fell nearly a story to the fan below.

Draped against the blades, I felt my arms and hands tingle. My butt slipped between the blades and my body folded in half. I barely had time to question what was beneath me before I slipped away into the darkness below.

Rats

I didn't remember passing out, but I assumed from the pain in my head I had collided with something hard. I blinked away the blur in my vision and took in my new surroundings.

The bridge of this ship was nothing like my small cockpit. It had a proper room devoted to its flight command and mechanical management. A lengthy console with multiple chairs sat beneath a massive view window that likely doubled as a navigation screen. The set up allowed for the option of dividing duties up between several crew members rather than just the pilot.

"Ah, there, see." Reynard's nostrils came into view, blocking out everything around me. "No need to worry. She's fine." He pulled at my eyelids, forcing them to open farther. Light blinded me as a flashlight jumped from one eye to the other.

I swatted away his invasive observations. When I found my arms to be fully functional, I shifted my legs to test them out as well. Relieved to be free from my atrophied muscles, I jumped up.

I fell as quickly as I stood, hitting the floor beside the work station I had been laying on. I shoved Reynard to one side, partially to steady myself, and partially to get him the hell away from me.

I stood again and caught sight of Terrin and Ayil standing on the other side of the room. Besides their lacking wardrobes, they were each donning a pair of manacles. As dizziness set in, the room spun, and I spun with it—taking in my surroundings.

I saw another familiar face, and I stopped to stare at him. "Mr. Davis?" I stumbled toward him. First one step, then two, then a running leap. I wasn't sure what sound erupted from my mouth, perhaps a war cry, but it was enough to make the man shift into immediate reverse. I shoved my fist into his face. Too disorientated to aim, I barely nicked his chin with my knuckles.

"Miss Mallory!" Reynard yelled. "There is no reason for violence."

"I said you should have put her in cuffs," Mr. Davis grumbled as he shuffled away from me. I shifted gears, turning my angry gaze to Reynard. Skipping the war cry, I moved back to him. The room had stilled and my steps were becoming more precise. There was no question what my diminishing distance was leading up to, but Reynard didn't run from me.

"Oh, now, now." Reynard waved his hands as if his words controlled my physical fury.

I threw my fist at him. Reynard was a little shorter, so there was barely a need to aim. Any random extension of my arm was bound to hit him. Or so I thought.

On impact, my hand bounced off his face like rubber. The familiar twinkle of a hidden shield lit across his face. I frowned. I would not get my revenge. Reynard shrugged apologetically. "I invented it, remember? I certainly use it."

I glared at him, cradling my aching hand. Rubber or not, he was still flesh and blood. I pressed the button below my chin. Like a second skin, the shield seeped over my face. I grabbed Reynard by the shoulders and pulled him forward as I threw myself forward.

"No, no, no!" Reynard babbled as my forehead came at him for a head butt.

I wanted to get a good bump on his noggin', even if it was at the expense of my own. However, I wasn't thinking straight. A shield in any form was still just energy. Variables of frequency, strength, and vibration to produce a static tension of atomic mass. And when two such energies meet.

Boom!

My head whipped back, and my body went flying with it. I was fortunate that I wasn't very strong or I might have decapitated myself. My whip-lashing impact sent me across the room with arms wheeling.

Someone broke my fall and kept me from the pleasure of a second concussion. I wriggled on top of his chest, debating on whether to elbow him in the ribs. I was at present running on the assumption of a blanket bad-guy status for anyone not in handcuffs. However, becoming a human pinball exhausted my desire for violence. Not to mention my short stint of boxing had wounded me more than I preferred to admit. I didn't even know if I was winning or losing.

I rolled off the man beneath me and kneeled on the floor for a moment to take an inventory of my missing brain cells. Across the bridge, I could see that Reynard had taken quite a tumble himself. Mr. Davis helped him off the floor.

I looked at Terrin and Ayil apologetically. I was always such a disappointing heroine when it came down to the physical stuff. The snarl on Ayil's face gave me pause until I realized he wasn't pointing it at me, but the lackey beside me. Terrin's jaw was also tensed, eyes narrowed, on the goon I had landed on. I turned to see what the no-name minion had done to offend them, but, as it turned out, he had a name.

"Rayne!" I rejoiced and leaned over to hug him. He reciprocated with a pat on my back. It wasn't until I leaned back that I suspected something was wrong.

I had thought Rayne was down on the planet, waiting for me to save him. Yet, there he was, clean-shaven and showered, dressed in all black. Apparently, someone else had already saved him. "How did you get here?"

He said nothing, but the look on his face was apologetic. As if he knew I wouldn't like the answer. Rayne stood up and helped me off the floor.

"I purchased him," Reynard said. "Or rather, Mr. Davis purchased him."

I looked back at Reynard. "You bought him? So, what, he's your slave now?"

"Don't be ridiculous." Reynard frowned. "He's my employee."

"You've hired him? Don't tell me, your personal bodyguard." I felt an icy grip on my wrists and looked down to see Rayne clasping two metal cuffs on each of my wrists. I looked up at him, seeing the sad determination on his face.

"It's just a precaution," he whispered quietly.

I gawked at him, barely understanding anything except that my husband was taking part in my capture. I suddenly realized why Terrin and Ayil were staring daggers at him. He must have been the one to put their cuffs on, as well.

"He's one of them, Kit," Ayil snarled.

I stared at Rayne, trying to put it together. Even as I tried to retrace my steps, I couldn't quite find the right puzzle pieces that made all of it make sense.

"Mr. Turner is not my bodyguard." Reynard went on in the conversation, oblivious to my world crashing. "I mean, he has been useful to us in that capacity from time to time, but not for me. As you can see, I don't need protection. However, I do need money to support my inventive process. So, to help pay the bills, I occasionally outsource Mr. Turner as a bodyguard when needed."

I shook my head and looked at Reynard. Somewhere in the conversation, he had lost me. "Mr. Turner?"

Reynard grimaced and hissed. "I admit the names got a little muddy over the decade before last."

"Decade before last?" A gaped at Rayne, realizing that this employment wasn't just a recent development. He knew Reynard from before his coma.

"Rayne Baloch is synonymous with power across the universe," Reynard continued. "Mr. Davis and Mr. Turner, however, are the face of that power. People often merge the name to the face they see, so the identities become flexible."

"How long has this man been in your employ, Captain?" I asked.

"Oh, good gracious, not counting the time we thought he was dead, maybe..." Reynard crinkled his face. "Nearly seven years." I took a step away from Rayne, observing the finely crafted black uniform he was wearing. I recognized the slim-fitting design of very expensive projectile proof fabric—not unlike what the biomechanoids wore. The outfit also had small pockets that lined his belly and thighs. Just big enough to holster knives—his preferred weapon.

"And what task was Mr. Turner assigned to do for you, Captain?"

Rayne glanced at Reynard as if asking permission to answer for himself. "After I made a name for myself in the dogfights, Captain Reynard bought me my freedom. He saw potential in my skills. He arranged my release in exchange for my services. Until my sleep lock, I was working as his personal assassin."

Personal

Personal assassin.

Rayne wasn't just a freelance assassin. He was being pimped out by Captain Reynard—the godfather of the universe. Why had that never come up? He had told me all the jarring details of his miserable childhood and tormented young adulthood. Why stop there?

Did he have to stop? Anonymity was no doubt part of his employment agreement. But why did he keep his pseudonym? I wondered if Turner was even his real name. Everyone from his past called him Rayne, but that may have been at his request.

I didn't have the answers to any of my questions. Especially the answers that I was interested in at the moment: loyalty and love. Where did his loyalty to Captain Reynard begin and his love for me end? Or better yet, had it ever begun?

I looked down at the cold metal brackets holding my wrists at a constant four-and-a-half-inch distance. I didn't know what was going on. First, I was being attacked. Then I was being saved. Then I was being contained. Now I was just a plain ole prisoner.

I didn't even know how to feel. The emotions were lying in wait, trying to decipher the stimuli before they activated.

There was only one thing that I was sure of. I was standing on the bridge of a strange ship, without my shirt and surrounded by five men. Three of whom I didn't know very well at all.

I bit back whatever pain was keeping me stunned and motioned my head toward Terrin and Ayil. "Release them," I demanded, with authority I wasn't sure anyone recognized. "And me." I raised my hands to Rayne. "We are leaving."

Rayne looked at my wrists, but made no attempt to undo the restraints.

"You've saved our lives, Captain. I'm assuming you don't wish me dead. If you wish to protect my DNA, then turn me over to the empire."

"Sanders is long gone now," Reynard said.

"Then release Terrin's shuttle and we will fly to the nearest outpost." I started moving to the exit. Terrin and Ayil took the hint and headed that way as well.

"Ooh, um," Reynard ran after me and blocked my progress, gingerly placing his hands on my arms. "I'm afraid I can't allow that."

"Are you holding the heir to the queen's throne captive, Captain Reynard?"

Reynard's face crumpled, and he let out a groan. "Now, why do you have to go and label everything? Can't we just invite you to stay for a while?"

"How long?"

"We'll play it by ear," he dithered.

"If it's an invitation, then we can decline. And FYI, invites don't come with shackles." I nodded to Ayil and Terrin. Ayil graciously raised his bound hands, displaying two middle fingers.

Reynard took a breath, frustrated by my rejection. "Okay, fine, you are a prisoner." He threw up his hands and stepped away. "Are you happy now?" His face muddled with surprising menace. "We'll just all carry on like a bunch of uncivilized brutes! Punching each other and insulting each other! Never mind polite conversation—"

"You are holding me against my will!"

"I am protecting the universe," Reynard seethed and pushed back into my space. "I was told that you are a compassionate woman. That you wish for the welfare of others above yourself. Is that untrue?"

I eased myself away from him. "I do."

Reynard took a threatening step back to me and pressed his face uncomfortably close to mine. "Then you must take my word that you being here is in the interest of many. I rarely make threats, Miss Mallory, but I assure you that I do have a contingency plan for you. If your DNA becomes impossible to contain, then it will need to be *destroyed*."

I glanced at Rayne and found that he was shaking his head slightly and giving me a stern look. A warning perhaps. Reynard wasn't a big man, nor was he likely to get physical with me, but he could, no doubt, find an inventive way to kill me, should he deem it necessary.

"I am the most influential man in the universe. My technology can win wars, overthrow governments, and capsize any disagreeable financial institutions. I've done it before and I can do it again, like that." Reynard snapped his fingers.

"Here you are, standing on my ship, in the very same room with me, and you cast away my invitation like I'm some M87 begging you for money." The glimmer in Reynard's eyes was unexpectedly frightening. "If my reputation isn't enough to lure your obedience, then perhaps we should rewind your memory to the ship you purchased from Mr. Davis."

I glanced at Mr. Davis, wondering how that had anything to do with this moment—except, of course, that it was Reynard's ship that was sold to me. His weapons' system. His technology, not Rayne's. Mr. Davis wasn't buying a random ship. He had come to retrieve his boss's tech before it landed in the wrong hands. I had always assumed that it was the depth of my credit stamp that had influenced Mr. Davis to sell it to me, but it was more complicated than that.

"You've already benefited from my generosity once, Princess. One might even say that you owe me for your new life." Reynard raised his finger in thought. "And just in case you still feel burdened by my request, perhaps I should point out that you have been using my personal assassin as your personal bodyguard. So maybe it's time you showed me some of that respect I was looking for earlier."

Five minutes earlier, if someone had asked me to describe Captain Reynard, I might have called him clownish and scattered. Now, feeling his breath on my face and staring into his stony eyes, I felt he needed an additional description: unhinged.

"What do you want?" I asked.

"Get comfortable with your new home," Reynard specified. "We have a lot to discuss."

I looked back at Terrin to confirm my assessment of our situation. He nodded slightly, giving me permission to knuckle under. At least for the time being. "Can we at least get some clothes?"

Reynard's snarl disappeared, quickly replaced by a shy smile, as he noticed my exposed bra. "Of course." As sincere as his embarrassment appeared to be, I found his mercurial mood just as disconcerting as his volatility.

Stranger

There had been plenty of dire moments in my life. Times when I didn't quite know what to do or say to get myself out of the predicament I was in. I always figured it out, though. Found a way to get free or save myself. Granted, I usually just got tangled in my web of problems even tighter, but I had to start somewhere.

As I walked down the long corridor behind Rayne, Ayil, and Terrin, I couldn't think of a time that I was more unsure of myself. If the man leading me wasn't my husband, Terrin and Ayil, would be silently plotting their attack on him. Once he was subdued, I would grab the pistol on his thigh and start shooting until I hit something critical enough to be useful.

But he was my husband—or was he? His name wasn't even his. I wasn't even sure if Turner was his real name.

The part of me that regretted indulging in a relationship with a man I barely knew was now screaming, I told you so! I still couldn't put my finger on where it had all gone wrong. Was any of it real?

I really had the worst taste in men.

Rayne stopped in front of one of the many doors lining the hall and typed in a code. The door lock released, and he nodded for Ayil to go in.

"Are you seriously not going to say anything?" Ayil asked. "You're just going to stand there and do those bastards' bidding."

"Rey is eccentric and a little paranoid, but he isn't going to hurt you."

"He shot me with an electrified leash."

"I know there isn't a lot of wiggle room for personality differences after something like that, but that was Rey's version of a practical joke."

"Almost killing me was funny to him."

"No, he never had any intention of killing you. Trust me, if Rey wanted you dead, you would be."

"How is that comforting right now?" Ayil asked.

"You're going to have to trust me on this."

"Sure thing, Mr. Turner." Ayil lifted his restraints and Rayne entered a sequence for them. The device had only just clicked when Ayil ripped his hands out and grabbed Rayne by the throat. Terrin leaped forward, but it was difficult to say if he was holding Ayil back or facilitating shoving Rayne into the wall. Terrin unholstered Rayne's pulse pistol and aimed it at his face. I looked around, frantically trying to play catch up for my part in our escape. Doors, doors, and more doors. All locked, I was sure.

"You are a liar!" Ayil squeezed Rayne's throat hard, making him cough. "How can we trust anything you say?"

Rayne pulled a knife from out of one of his many pockets and held it to Ayil's neck. "You'll bleed out long before I suffocate," Rayne rasped through his grip.

"And this pulse pistol will take out half your face," Terrin said.

Rayne used his free hand to tap his forehead, which flickered slightly with the energy of a shield. "No, it won't." Between that and his energy resistant clothing, Rayne was effectively bulletproof.

Ayil grumbled and pulled away from Rayne. Terrin lowered the gun, not willing to continue with the losing battle. Rayne snatched the pulse pistol from his hand. Terrin smiled at him. "I hardly need it to hurt you."

"You're right, you don't need it, because, as I've said before, you are not in any danger." Rayne holstered the pistol.

"Then perhaps you'd like to explain why we have been brought here. Why does there seem to be some discrepancy about your name?"

"I think we'd all like an answer to that one," I said.

Rayne glanced at me, a little of his guilt pushing through his general irritation. "As far as anyone is concerned, Rayne Baloch is a weapons designer and an infamous assassin and a savvy investor. They are all the same man in the rumors. The man I used to be died in the dogfights, long ago. That was the condition of my purchase price and my freedom. I became Mr. Turner and never looked back. I don't expect you to understand." Rayne set his eyes on me, now unapologetic for his casual deception. "I've been honest about my origins except for my connection to Mr. Davis and our employer."

"Why?" Terrin asked. "Why was that detail left out?"

Rayne looked at Terrin. "Because I had an obligation to him. He is a very sought after man. I couldn't risk telling you about him. As far as the universe is concerned, he is a ghost."

"Did you really think that we would tell someone about him?" I asked.

"Not voluntarily."

"But why didn't—," I began.

"Because it's what I did, Kit!" Rayne's unapologetic eyes were now cold and remorseless. "I made a choice to maintain the identity that I was accustomed to."

I took a breath, not willing to take my scolding lying down, but he wasn't leaving any room for argument. "And now that you're back with him? What now? Get back into the swing of being his personal assassin?"

"Oh, I'm sorry. I wasn't aware that there was a difference between being his personal assassin and being yours."

"I've never asked you to kill anyone."

"Yes, you did, the minute you asked an assassin to be your bodyguard. Or did you think I would just negotiate with the men and women putting guns and knives on you?"

"I'll be sure to add that to my list of bad life choices. Including sleeping with you." Rayne's expression turned murky, a blend of all sorts of anger and pain.

"As necessary as this argument might be," Terrin interrupted, placing a hand on my shoulder. "I think we should focus on the moment. Why is Captain Reynard insistent that he has to protect the universe from Kit?"

Rayne's expression softened slightly, and his eyes drifted back to me. "Because... you aren't what you think you are."

TRAITOR

"You mean I don't have special DNA?" I asked after Rayne delivered Ayil to his quarters to rest and dress.

"It's not quite that simple." Rayne opened the next door for Terrin and motioned for him to enter.

Terrin examined the room carefully before looking back at me. Rayne motioned his thumb to the room again, but Terrin didn't move. "I'm not leaving her side."

"I'm not going to hurt her," Rayne seethed.

Terrin's lip tipped up slightly and he stepped into the frame of the door. He turned his head to look at Rayne. "You already have," he said before entering.

Rayne slammed his hand on the controls and the door closed. He waited a moment before turning and ushering me down the hall again. "Rey isn't even a biologist," he said as we walked down the corridor a little farther. "He considers you more of a..."

"Hobby?"

"I was going to say a curiosity," Rayne smirked at me. "He just has to dispel a few concerns regarding your creation."

"My creation?" I asked, wondering when my miraculous birth had suddenly become a science experiment. Granted, it was never too far from that to begin with, but I wasn't quite a test-tube baby. My parents conceived me naturally—albeit under the duress of sociopolitical pressure.

Rayne frowned and even had the gall to look me up and down—and not in a flirtatious way. "You always told me that you were a cloistered child. You never really left your homes."

"Right."

"Do you think that was normal?"

"As compared to what? According to my mother, royalty should live and die inside the walls of the palace. To her, I was a world traveler."

"What about... the tests?" Rayne didn't look at me when he asked the question. I tried to hide my surprise, but my feet slowed to a stop. He turned to me, looking squeamish, like the subject wasn't his choice to discuss. I wondered at that moment if I was being interrogated. Was Captain Reynard the one steering this conversation?

"How do you know about that?" I asked rather than deny the tests he was referring to. In truth, I had never thought much about my Saturday morning routine. It was just something that I did while I was on my father's planet. It was rarely anything more than a physical exam. Occasionally, they would take blood or saliva. Once in a while, they required urine. Sometimes, my doctor simply conversed with me. From my perspective, it was an excuse to get out of the house. I even missed the routine while I was at my mother's, but she refused to have anyone other than her dedicated physicians in our home. Plus, even she thought weekly examinations were excessive.

"It's like Reynard said. He's been monitoring you for a long time."

"And you? Is that what you have been doing? Monitoring me?"

Rayne scoffed and rolled his eyes. "Oh, you would love that, wouldn't you?"

"Love what?"

"You would love for me to be the bad guy in this."

I raised my restrained hands. "Aren't you the one that put these on me?"

"Because you almost blew your head off. I can't trust you."

"Yes, that's something we have in common."

"Don't! Don't turn this on me just because I neglected a few minor details about my past."

"Your name is a minor detail?" I squawked.

"I've had dozens of names, Kit. Every planet is a new identity when you're an assassin. You assumed I was Rayne because that's who I was when I went to sleep on that ship. When I woke up, I was still coming to terms with a ten-year gap in my memory. And in case you forgot, I barely had a chance to meet you before Terrin dragged you back home to Brahama."

"Then what?"

"What?"

I crossed my arms and gave him a double-dog dare glare. "I know Ayil wanted to save me, but what was your motivation to join the ranks of hero."

Rayne seemed to realize his predicament. I was figuring out his real motivations—as guided by his former/current employer. Rayne twisted his lips, but finally grumbled out the truth. "After I got in contact with him again, he suggested that I assist with your rescue. Reynard preferred having you away from your mother and father."

"Why?" I asked flatly. I had reached a steady thrum of anger, so there was no point in yelling. I needed answers more than a needed emotional release.

"He didn't specify, and I didn't ask."

"Was sleeping with me at his request too?" I didn't keep the anger out of my voice that time.

Rayne turned slowly to look at me. His shock stemmed from my accusation of prostitution, on top of coercion and impersonation. Ire flashed in his eyes as he approached me, but before I could flinch away from any potential physical reproach, his gaze had turned sly. He pressed into my space, looming over me. He whispered. "You crawled into my bed, Kit. Don't you forget that."

"Why did you leave?" I locked eyes with him, refusing to let him turn our impromptu love affair into something romantic when it was only ever something convenient. "Did Reynard order you to kill Helana?"

Rayne shook his head. "I knew Terrin was about to blow my cover. We decided that my exit was for the best. I planned to meet up with Rey later. Helana was still my revenge plot. I never expected you to follow me. Certainly not twice."

"Your boss must have been pleased I invited you back, despite your resume."

Rayne raised his hand, pushing my chin up so he could run his hand along my neck down to my exposed neckline. I had forgotten about my lacking shirt until then. "I was glad that you invited me back."

I shook my head slightly and swallowed hard.

"What do you think, Kit? Do you think every kiss was choreographed? Every touch?" He moved his hand lower, skirting his fingers along the fabric of my bra. "Do you honestly think that Reynard instructed me on how to make you come?" Rayne wrapped his arm around me and pulled me against him. He placed his hand behind my head and pulled me into a heated kiss. He pinched my ass and pushed me back into the wall of the hallway. I was certain that if unbound, I would have wrapped my arms around him and ridden out the passion of the moment like a proper exhibitionist. As it was, though, the handcuffs were digging into my side. I had shifted my hands to allow Rayne to press against me as he desired. The more he ground against me, trying to appease the heat growing inside of him, the more I felt a frosty storm brewing in my mind.

It wasn't about the lie or lies. It was about loyalty. Rayne may have had a legitimate attraction to me, and maybe his love was honest too, but he had no devotion to me. He was committed to his employer. The only influence I had over him was on the level of tension in his pants.

I reached around for his pistol. It was resting in his waistband where it belonged, but I could get it out before he noticed. He wore the same face shield as Reynard, and the anti-static material in his uniform was almost impossible to burn through. However, I also knew that pulse pistol discharges at close proximity were difficult to disperse across the material. Regardless of the uniform's protection level, Rayne was going to feel it.

Kachoo!

The gentle noise didn't sound like the gunfire of a shrapnel weapon. It was more like an electric stapler.

And yet, the discharge was enough to incapacitate most humanoids with one shot.

Rayne's lips and hands receded from me instantly. He bent over and cradled his crotch. I hadn't intended to shoot him there, but I didn't have much room to aim. Rayne groaned, but even as he noticed his pistol clasped between my cuffed hands, his moan turned into a feral roar.

I must've disappointed him because he didn't hold back his strength when he returned to defend himself. His movements were lightning fast. I didn't even realize what was happening until he pinned me against the wall, his body pressed to mine. This time, my hands were above my head and he was viciously twisting the gun from my grasp.

I yelped as my wrist got torqued, but I didn't let go and neither did he. Gripped firmly in both my hands, I had no intention of surrendering the weapon.

"I can't believe you just did that," Rayne said through gritted teeth, his hot breath on my cheek and neck.

"I thought today was the day for surprises." I tried to squirm out of his grip, but he just pushed back, pressing himself against me harder.

"Drop the gun, Kit." Seeing no hope against his strength, I tossed the pistol away. It clambered to the floor. As I predicted, Rayne released his grip on me and immediately reached down to pick it up. Unsatisfied with my first little revolution, I kicked him in the throat while he bent over to grab it.

Rayne stumbled back, cursing at me. Just to piss him off, I dove to retrieve the pistol again. I picked it up, rolled over, and aimed it. Unfortunately, Rayne was done playing. He kicked it out of my hands, sending it skittering down the hall, well out of our reach.

I still wasn't ready to give up, so I punched him in the crotch. Since he was already in pain from the discharge, the additional impact made him cough and sputter.

"Goddammit, Kit!" Rayne backpedaled away to protect himself from further damage.

Anticipating his incapacitation for at least a few seconds, I scrambled across the floor to recover the pistol. Once I had in hand, I jumped to my feet and whipped around to fire at Rayne. His barreling tackle sent me back to the floor with him on top of me. The gun popped from my hand and slid further down the hall.

Rayne didn't waste any time trying to calm me down. He pulled himself off the floor and yanked me up behind him. He ducked down and bent me over his shoulder to carry me to my containment.

Despite a few fists to his back, he got me into the room and threw me on the bed. He pressed a button to shut the door, leaving me alone inside. I moved back to the door and tried to open it, but he had locked it.

I was trapped.

I was a prisoner... again.

Out of the Fire

"Helloooo." Reynard's voice pierced my dreams. "Push the button, sweetheart."

I hadn't remembered falling asleep. I blinked, looking for the source of the irritating voice. I saw a light flashing through my hooded lids. I shifted off the bed, relieved to find my wrists free of their shackles. I moved to the blinking button on the panel beside the door. I pushed the insistent red dot and Reynard's image popped up on the tiny screen. His face took up nearly the entire screen, affording me a good view of his nostrils.

"There you are. Had a little nap, did you? Good. Come upstairs, you're missing dinner."

I rubbed my eyes and shook my head. "I'm not hungry."

"Then come up for a drink." Reynard's bright expression dimmed slightly. "Please," he added.

"Captain, I'm not accustomed to entertaining in my undergarments."

Reynard's eyes drifted down and his brow dipped slightly, as if he once again failed to realize that my bra was not meant to be my entire torso wardrobe. "What?" Reynard glanced away from the screen. "Oh. There is a package outside your door—clothing. Get dressed and come up. Your men are already here." The image flickered and disappeared.

I pulled on the door handle and found it unlocked. On the floor outside, I found a small brown package. I picked it up and ripped it open. After nearly a minute of deciphering the outfit, I realized it was someone's idea of a joke.

Ten minutes later, I walked into the dining room sporting an outfit that could best be described as retro-futuristic. The two-toned off white and teal dress was a mixture of leather and mesh, with clear plastic-stacked shoulder pads. I appeared to be some hybridization of a punk rocker, a football player, and a prostitute. I couldn't tell if the purpose of the fashionable monstrosity was to make a statement or to torture anyone who saw it.

Though I had tried the outfit on several times, I had found no position that would prevent my breasts or ass from being exposed—therefore my bra was still on, as well as my pants, making the outfit that much more ridiculous.

All eyes looked up as I entered. Terrin and Ayil were speaking with our host Reynard. They each did a double take. Naturally, the clothing selected for them was dark-colored, slim-fitting, and, from the looks of the fabric, comfortable.

I heard a snort in the back of the room and found Mr. Davis nearly choking on his beverage. Rayne was next to him, his lips straining to maintain a thin smile against the smirk that was tugging his lip back. He coughed into his hand and looked away from me.

"Mademoiselle!" Reynard clapped his hands together and rushed over to me. "Thank you for joining us. Do come in." His eyes dragged down my body, taking in the ridiculous ensemble. "You know, I do find that I'm not as good at identifying fashion as other people. Is this what the ladies are wearing these days?"

"I hope not," I grumbled.

"Can I get you a drink?"

"What you can get me," I said, my volume poised for a shout, "is—"

"She'll have what I'm having." Terrin came over and gave me a sideways hug. He dodged my shoulder pads to kiss me on my cheek. "Let's just play along," he whispered in my ear.

I glanced up at him and gave Reynard a slight nod. "I'll have the same. Thank you." Reynard ran off to make my drink. "And what am I having?" I asked.

Terrin handed me his glass, and I took a sip. The sweet astringent taste was mildly alcoholic. "Yummy. I can't remember the last time I had a cocktail."

Terrin smiled warmly and looked around the room. "I can't remember the last time I've had a meal that didn't come prepackaged."

"What, no hydrated food?" I looked over the table of covered dishes that were currently cooking or cooling the impending meal.

"No, apparently besides a very expansive bar, our host has shipped in fresh fruits, vegetables, and a roasted pig."

"Good lord, I guess we can assume he has money to burn. Although, with Mr. Davis as his financial adviser, I'm not surprised." I gave Mr. Davis, who was still finding humor in my dress, a glare. "Please tell me you have an escape plan for dessert."

"Ayil and I were fortunate enough to get a tour of the ship before the cocktails. The Captain is an *interesting* character, I'll give him that. Judging by the technology on this ship, which is light years ahead of any military vessel I've seen, he is definitely a genius. However, he behaves like a spoiled child."

"Mmm, maybe I can relate to him," I said, stealing Terrin's drink for another sip.

"Despite being a one-man army, he doesn't come off like a politician or a soldier, though. He's more like a salesman."

"What's he selling?"

Terrin gave me a worried look. "Only enough to support his income and maintain his reputation. He's very proud of the mystique that surrounds him."

"Is he serious about felling governments and steering wars?"

"I think we should assume he is. Given what we know about Rayne's past, I think it would be easy to see how he could eliminate anyone that gets in the way of his plans."

"Brains, brawn, and a conniving rat. They make the perfect team."

I noticed Rayne eyeing us from across the room. Mr. Davis frowned at Terrin and asked Rayne a question. He didn't return his gaze, but I saw him mouth, *"I have no idea."*

"What did you find out from Rayne?" Terrin asked.

I frowned, disappointed that I hadn't gotten further in my interrogation before the kissing and shooting had gotten started. "Not much. There seems to be some interest in my Saturday morning appointments."

"Mmm," Terrin gave a noncommittal acknowledgment. He was well aware of my appointments. As my bodyguard, he had accompanied me to them many times. Though he waited outside during the actual examinations.

"Why do I suddenly feel like that pig that we're about to eat? Is there apple in my teeth?" I bared my teeth for him to check.

Terrin gave me a small smile for my effort to amuse him. Which was rather impressive, I thought. The alcohol must have been softening him up. "Don't worry, Mallory. I will not let anyone put you on a spit. However, Reynard is quite moody. I think it wise to appeal to his playful nature and avoid bruising his ego."

"Oh, but you know how much I love to bruise egos." I cocked an eyebrow, threatening to be the wrench in his plan.

Terrin stared down at me. I expected him to scold me with his eyes—demand my obedience, but there was a slight sparkle of delight in his eyes. He was definitely getting tipsy. "Do you want to know what my father thought of you?" he asked.

"Oh, good god, no." I blanched. "The last thing I need right now is to know how much your father hated me."

Terrin laughed. The deep sound was music to me, and I couldn't help smiling at him. For a moment, it really felt like we were just two people chatting at a cocktail party.

"Here we go." Reynard arrived suddenly with my drink, interrupting whatever Terrin wanted to tell me. I thanked him and took it. "And what are we talking about?"

Terrin shifted back, allowing Reynard space to be included in the conversation. "Mallory and I were just discussing some old business."

"Am I interrupting?"

"Not at all." Terrin rested a hand on Reynard's shoulder. "That's the thing about old business, it's never anything urgent and until it's resolved... it'll just be there waiting." Terrin gave me a knowing smile and even winked at me. I made a mental note to add alcohol to our future conversations. "If you'll excuse me, I think I need to go put out a fire." Terrin walked away and joined in on the *discussion* Ayil and Rayne were having across the room.

"Does he always call you Mallory?" Reynard asked.

I nodded, staring after my former bodyguard admiringly. His mere arrival into Rayne and Ayil's dispute was enough to ease the physical threat between them. "Terrin and I met while I was on my father's planet, so he only knew me as Mallory Kit."

"Everyone else calls you Kit, though, right?"

"Kit is fine. The only people that call me Mallory are Terrin and my father." My thoughts lingered a moment on my father. I was worried about him. I wondered what torture he had endured upon warning me to stay away from home. Returning to Vagari was out of the question, but witnessing the unrest in the government made me wonder if the fallout from of my freedom was worth it.

"Call me Rey. After Rayne took on my usual nickname, I had to switch to Rey. If he takes that, I guess I'll have to go by my middle name." Rey chuckled, and I joined in.

"What do you call him again?"

"Mr. Turner."

"What's his first name?"

"When I met him he was Alex Turner? We dropped the first name and designated him Mr. Turner. Last names give the impression of business only."

"In that case, I wish he would have introduced himself to me as Mr. Turner. Might have saved me some trouble."

Reynard frowned. "You know, I'm not the type of man to understand the carnal desires of men and women, but if I may intrude, and give you some knowledge of Mr. Turner."

"What's that?"

"Well, he tends to be very open with his heart and... such."

"Excuse me?"

"I don't mean that as a bad thing. I mean, it's true that Starla was an outright debacle and nearly got him killed, but he had a perfectly normal relationship with Kylin. And Veruca was... well, that one was a debacle too. My point is, he has a romantic side I could never squelch out."

I frowned. "Are you saying that Rayne is a pig?"

"No, just that whatever happened between you and Mr. Turner had nothing to do with me."

"Did he ask you to tell me that?"

Mr. Davis came up behind Reynard and tapped him on the shoulder. He whispered something in his ear. "Oh, speaking of pigs, the meal is almost ready. Would you excuse me?" Reynard scurried off to check the contents of one of his cooking platters, leaving me with Mr. Davis.

"I think this makes us even." Mr. Davis smirked at me.

"What makes us even?" Mr. Davis's eyes traced down my body, indicating my outfit. "You picked out this horrific thing?"

Mr. Davis nodded. "You didn't think I was gonna let that little punch go unanswered."

"Since when is the response to a sore chin a bad outfit?"

Mr. Davis circled behind me, swirling his drink and making the ice cubes clink in the glass. "Even if I were the type of man to... brawl." Mr. Davis said the word brawl as if it was something distasteful to his palate. "I know better than to touch any of Rayne's women."

I cringed at the idea of being one of Rayne's women. Like I was one in a long line of hobby girlfriends. According to Rey, I may well have been. "Oh really? If you're so worried about what Rayne would think of you brawling with me, I wonder what he would think about what you did to me down on the planet under the stadium?"

Mr. Davis lost his smirk for only a moment, but it was long enough to know that he didn't want that little secret to get out. "Princess, do you know what it is that your husband and I do for Rey?" I shook my head. "We make problems disappear. He does it with a flick of his wrist and a spray of blood. I do it with the careful management of monetary assets and information. I don't mean to flaunt my expertise, but you must understand that when we want something—we either buy it, trade for it, or take it. If you feel somehow cheated by our transaction, then I suggest you consider it a lesson for your future dealings. I did tell you not to let anyone know what you really want. It gives them power."

"The only power you have, Mr. Davis, is what Captain Reynard gives you. Those men at the dogfights that were threatened by your presence. They weren't afraid of you, they were afraid of your boss. You are just an errand boy.

Wheeling and dealing for the best price on cargo. You're a glorified personal shopper."

Mr. Davis's jaw rolled and his eyes narrowed. "I changed my mind. The outfit doesn't make us even. You should have stayed on my good side."

"You don't have a good side, Mr. Davis. You're a prophet monger and a money whore. I can't imagine a side of you that has any compassion or remorse."

"You might be right about that." Mr. Davis pinned me with his gaze. "You know, something you should consider. The fear that arrives in my wake may not be for me specifically, but it's not for Captain Reynard, either. That fear has been cultivated by rumors. Stories told and retold about a vicious assassin with no mercy for those who cross us." Mr. Davis simpered, delighted by my stupor. "If you really want to know what Rayne is capable of, just ask him who—"

"Dinner's ready." I jumped as Rayne approached us and looked between our uncivil expressions. "Everything okay here, Davis?"

Mr. Davis found his cheerful smile again and turned it on Rayne. "Yeah, no problem. You've quite a girl there." He slapped Rayne on the shoulder. "Quite a handful," he mumbled as he walked away.

Rayne glanced at me. "You okay." He reached up to touch my arm, but I pulled away.

"You want to crawl your way back into my good graces, Turner? Keep that man the hell away from me."

INTO THE FRYING PAN

I looked over the square table overflowing with steaming meat, buttery vegetables, and a stack of fruit that qualified as a meal and a centerpiece. Everyone took a seat, leaving me with the decision of sitting beside Rayne, Ayil, or Terrin. Since sitting next to Rayne or Ayil put me catty-corner to Mr. Davis or Rey, I opted to sit next to Terrin. Judging by the glare Rayne gave each of us, my choice had implied something different to him. Just to piss him off, I scooted my chair a little closer to Terrin. I blatantly stared right at my so-called husband as I did it, which prompted yet another level of fury to seep into his eyes.

Terrin was oblivious to the nerve that we were once again plucking at. He poured me a glass of ice water before handing the carafe over to Ayil on my right. As he leaned across me, I detected the smell of cologne. It surprised me, since he typically didn't wear a fragrance. Their lacking sweat glands left gattaw nearly odorless, so their culture had not developed the expansive perfumes and deodorants that humans had.

"So, Rey, are you actually a military captain or just titled for the sake of your vessel?" Terrin asked.

"Oh, I tried the military. Or rather, they tried me." Reynard snorted out his laughter and looked around to see if anyone caught the joke. Terrin let out a soft chuckle for the sake of the suck-up role.

"I take it the military didn't agree with you, or was it vice versa?" Terrin began loading up his plate with ample portions of meat and vegetables. After it was full, he cut a piece of his meat off and placed it on my plate. The act, although familiar to me, drew puzzled looks from the entire table.

"Both actually," Reynard said, recovering from the social oddity. "Well, mostly I didn't like them, but at some point, they tried to imprison me."

"Why did they do that?" Terrin asked as he carefully divided his brazed carrots to give me an exact one-third portion. Ayil scrunched his face at me and mouthed the question that was on the minds of everyone at the table. I just shook my head at him and rolled my eyes. I was beyond mortified to have Terrin publicly display the controlling behaviors of my childhood. He was apparently a good deal more drunk than I would have suspected or he would have realized how demeaning this was for me in adulthood.

"They wanted to keep me under control so I could keep making them weapons," Reynard continued. "I probably would have, but then I met someone who made me realize my brain was the real weapon, and I had to treat it as such."

Ayil took one of the citrus slices from his plate and passed it over to mine, mimicking Terrin's paternal actions. It made me smile, despite my embarrassment.

"You left the military to do what exactly?" Terrin asked Reynard.

"To create and expand my expertise in weapons engineering. I am years ahead of the existing regimes." Rey leaned forward as if to only speak across the table to me. "There was a time in my life when I was as hunted as you, my dear. Of course, that became less and less of a problem for me." Rey motioned broadly to his vessel. I couldn't help smiling at him. He really was like a ten-year-old child showing off his rock collection. Only instead of rocks, he had deadly weapons.

"And what do you do with your inventions?" Terrin continued his casual interrogation between bites of meat. "Surely, you aren't a salesman at heart."

"No, certainly not. I only sell my technology as needed, usually to small factions."

"Small factions? You mean rebels? Doesn't that create an imbalance in power?"

"That's the point, but I don't sell them more than they need to keep themselves independent, and they are given strict instructions on how to manage my tech."

"Manage it how?"

"There are rules when buying from me. I may create weapons that can win wars, but they could just as easily be used to colonize half the universe or worse yet, genocide."

"And these groups *always* follow your rules."

Rey snorted out a laugh again. "The smart ones do."

"Rey isn't exactly the type of guy you want to piss off," Mr. Davis added before taking a bite of his meat. "None of us are." He kept his eyes on me, driving home his point.

Terrin caught on to the subtle threat and looked at us. "I'm sure that goes for us as well, Mr. Davis." Mr. Davis turned his smug gaze to Terrin. He may not have considered him a threat earlier, but now that he was out of his handcuffs, it was a different story. "Which brings me to my next question." Terrin returned his gaze to Rey. "One that I feel has not fully been addressed—at least not to my satisfaction."

"And what is that?" Rey asked, glancing around at the tense faces around him.

"You've indicated that this arrangement is in Mallory's best interest. However, I am curious what your end game is?"

"End game?" Rey asked.

"I assume that a man of your distinction isn't in the habit of playing hero to damsels in distress. And judging by your business acumen, I also assume that you don't do favors out of the goodness of your heart. So…" Terrin leaned back and rested his arm on the back of my chair. "What do you want with Mallory?"

Rey put on a cockeyed smile and shrugged as if the answer should have been obvious. "The same as it's always been. To keep her genetic potential safe from those who would seek to use it for oppression, warfare, or pestilence."

I cringed, thinking about how others might use my DNA for pestilence. Was I even more naïve than I thought? I had always assumed the ultimate goal was to cure disease. I hadn't considered that someone might use genetic knowledge to cause disease.

After shoving away my visions of a zombie apocalypse, I tried to speak demurely. "Is there any reason that my mother's army couldn't keep me from spreading turmoil across the universe?"

Reynard sighed and put down his fork. He looked at his men before pinning me with a look that reminded me of my father—when he didn't want to deliver bad news to me. "There's a rather specific reason that I don't want you to return to your mother's care, but I'm not sure now is the time to discuss it."

My body tensed with anger and my mouth opened to once again rant about my captivity, but Terrin shifted his hand to rest on my shoulder. He pulled me back against the chair and gave me a gentle squeeze. I gave up on my argument and let Terrin continue with his slow progression of casual interrogation.

"I thought you said that you've been monitoring Mallory," Terrin asked, his words primed with bait.

"I have." Rey looked at me. "I met you as a baby—you obviously wouldn't remember, but I did."

I now voluntarily pushed myself back in my chair—readily accepting Terrin's domineering grip—so long as it provided protection against my creepy stalker. His grip on my shoulder eased a bit, but in its place, his thumb rubbed the nape of my neck. I wasn't sure if his intention was to relax me or distract me, but either way, I lost interest in the conversation.

"You were adorable, by the way," Rey went on. "Big cheeks and little fingers. You had—"

"You should know that Mallory is an adaptable woman. I haven't seen her shy away from a challenge yet. Well... maybe one." Terrin glanced at me and flashed a sly smile and wink before returning his attention back to Reynard. I barked out the start of a stunted laugh before containing my amusement at Terrin's rarely seen playfulness. "Captain, I appreciate that you want to spare Mallory's feelings, but I think you'll find that lies will never earn you any points with her."

I glanced at Rayne to see what he thought of that statement. He must have recognized the passive-aggressive dig, because his eyes were boring into the side of Terrin's head. Or maybe they had been there already.

Rey nodded. "I have no intention of lying to Mallory, but I do have a confession to make. The military service I referred to earlier... was with the Coalition." My attention on Rayne faded as I took a renewed interest in the conversation. "I worked in their R&D department for many years. I created the design that you now know as the biomechanoids. I and Dr. Alvin Kessler combined our sciences to turn dead men into zombie machines."

Everyone lowered their heads at this revelation—even Rayne and Davis, who likely already knew this story, turned their gaze downward. The repulsion for the biomechanoids was nearly universal. Unfortunately, they were too damn valuable for the Coalition to retire. I imagined Rey considered himself to be in line with historic men like Hitler, Teller, and Oppenheimer.

"After I saw what was happening... after I understood what we had created, I left the Coalition, and so did Kessler—eventually. I have been working toward protecting the universe from the Coalition's control. Dismantling any financial or political allies that might give them unequal power. I've even helped out your mother's military once or twice. A choice that almost bit me in the ass with General Sanders."

"You're making amends for you sins?" I asked. "Good for you. I can see why you would be so concerned about me falling into the wrong hands. My DNA could be used to make the Coalition's next super soldier?"

Rey shook his head. "No, dear, that's not what I'm afraid of. Your DNA is not leading to perfection, as you were told. It's leading to annihilation."

"Excuse me?" I glanced at Rayne to see if this man was just having a senior moment, but he wouldn't look at me. He just stared at his plate, not willing to face me, to give me the truth that he undoubtedly already knew. "What are you talking about?"

"Sweetheart, the prophecy is a lie. You are not a genetic miracle. You were designed and created by the Coalition. You're a weapon."

A Real Girl?

Heat pushed into my body and I felt faint. Reynard continued to speak. "You were genetically designed by Dr. Kessler. He was—"

"That's a lie!" I slammed my fist down on the table, making the glassware vibrate. "I was born to Richard Kit and Queen—"

"Yes, yes, born, but first your embryo was created through a very complex gene-splicing procedure." Reynard insisted.

"I don't believe you." I jumped from my chair, ready to physically fight for my birthright if necessary. "It was a natural conception. Those were the rules."

"Rules, Kit?" Rayne scoffed. "Do you hear yourself right now? Do you really think that was the one thing they left to chance?" I assumed he was trying to be diplomatic, but the attitude in his tone made me want to throw him in an airlock and jettison him into space.

"I am not a weapon!" I yelled at everyone. Terrin and Ayil were staring at me, just as shocked as me by this rendition of my existence. "I'm a..." I looked down at myself, half-expecting to see biomechanoid parts popping out of my flesh. "I'm... human," I whispered, now unsure of even that.

"Oh, no, no, of course, you are human," Rey explained. "No one is contesting that."

"Then how can I be a weapon? Why would they even do that to me?"

Rey took a breath and spoke with genuine compassion. "The peace between the Coalition and the empire was always tenuous. The Coalition continued to strive for universal dominance, but they knew as long as the empire was loyal to a sovereign leader, they would never have control. Secretly, they plotted against the queen, trying to devise any way they could to take control. Kessler was the first to suggest that we overthrow the empire from within. It was genius, really. A war without a war.

"The religious rhetoric that so much of the empire held dear became the foundation for his plot. It allowed for a meaningful proposition while veiling the child's creation under the flag of diplomacy. You were toted as the olive branch between the two nations. Since your mother still needed an heir, it was an easy sell. Frankly, I think she liked the idea of a politically approved child."

"How am I supposed to overthrow a government?"

"You aren't. I mean, not anymore. You're already past your..." Rey clasped his hands together. "Hmm, how shall I put this? You were supposed to die when you were sixteen."

"What?" My dizziness seemed to shift down into my stomach where it upset the balance of my meal.

"Your purpose was to be a carrier. On your sixteenth birthday, you were meant to deliver a deadly virus to Brahama. You were designed to..." Rey rose to his feet. "Do you want to sit down? You're looking a little pallid."

"No." I shook my head. "Go on."

Rey frowned. "You were designed to assassinate your mother."

I could no longer hold my eyes on anything. The table before me was just a blur of colors. I couldn't feel my feet even as they moved me away from the table. I wasn't sure where I was going, but I had to be away from the eyes that were watching me, gauging me, and judging me.

"Does…" I heard Ayil start to speak and stop. He started again, quieter. "Does her father know she is a weapon?"

My head whipped around to stare at Reynard. Anger surged inside of me as I waited for him to speak even one disparaging word about my father. He noted my stare and shook his head. "I don't know for certain."

"No!" I straightened my stance and returned to the table. "He never would have been part of something so conniving. My father is a good man." The more I thought about my father and his gentle nature, the more I realized that this entire plot was wrong. "This is all bullshit! I don't believe a word of this! You are just manipulating me and trying to conflict my loyalties. You are the saboteurs and spies!"

"If you don't believe us," Rayne said smugly, "just ask him." He turned his blooming sneer on Terrin.

I looked at Terrin, who had a snarl aimed back at Rayne. "Ask him what?"

Rayne chuckled and crossed his arms. "Come on, Kit, don't be this naïve. Don't you think he knew what you were?"

I looked between Terrin and Rayne. Terrin's jaw clenched tight as he stared Rayne down, but he wasn't offering any objection to any suggestion of prior knowledge.

"When did Terrin come into your life again?" Rayne asked with feigned curiosity. "Wasn't it around fifteen?"

"Yes," I answered.

"And why was he assigned to you?"

I took a few labored breaths and looked at Ayil for help, but he seemed just as intrigued by Rayne's train of thought as I was. "He was supposed to keep away disfavourable lovers."

"Disfavourable lovers?" Rayne stood slowly and circled the table. "In the mansion that you hardly ever left and the palace where you were kept under lock and key? Who were these talented miscreants who could get past multiple armed men warranting the need for a dedicated bodyguard?"

I licked my lips and looked at Terrin. He was finally looking at me. Staring at me was more like it. "My father wanted..."

"Your father didn't hire him, the Coalition did. Isn't that right, Terrin?" Rayne put his hands on Terrin's shoulders and gave him a shake. He turned slowly to glare at him before looking back at me. I couldn't place his demeanor. He didn't look guilty. If anything, he looked at be the one accusing me of doing something wrong. "And what were his rules, Kit?"

I shook my head and took another step away from the table. I didn't want to think anymore. I may have been an adaptable woman, but Rayne had already broken my heart. I couldn't take a betrayal from Terrin.

"Sleeping habits? Eating habits?" Rayne leaned past Terrin and flicked the edge of my plate, making it lift and smack down loudly on the table. "Since when do bodyguards give a damn about your healthy lifestyle?"

Rayne moved between Terrin and me, mostly obstructing my view of him. "Did you know that gattaw can't get sick from human diseases? They are virtually impervious to even our most deadly viruses."

Rayne shifted back to include Terrin in the conversation again. "How long was your service supposed to be?" Despite his subdued reaction to Rayne's taunts, Terrin's shoulders were rising and falling from heavy breaths. "Go on. Tell her the truth. We all know what the answer is, anyway."

Terrin rolled his jaw before speaking. "The contract was described as self-eliminating following a one-year service."

"So, shortly after she arrived at Brahama, your services would no longer be required?"

"Yes."

"What a coincidence?"

"You knew?" I asked Terrin in a whisper. His eyes shot back to me and he glared as if I was the one betraying him.

"Of course, he knew." Rayne slapped his back before sidling up next to me. "I'm not the only man who has lied to you," he whispered in my ear before heading back to his seat to finish his meal.

For a moment, I just stood there, staring at Terrin. He watched me; a certain disappointment reflecting on me. I sensed that even if I accused him of plotting against me, the only backlash would be his stoic resolve to maintain loyalty to his employer. At that time, his oath meant everything to him. And I meant very little to him.

Rather than endure the torture of one of Terrin's lectures, I didn't question him. Though he seemed to beg for a fight from me, this was one time I couldn't bring myself to confront him.

I sat back down on the edge of my seat, trying to keep my distance from Terrin, as I took a tentative sip of my drink. When the sip turned into a long draw, I found the bottom of the glass much too soon. I returned to the bar and found something that tasted well enough to guzzle and returned to my seat. Terrin looked at my spilling glass of liquor as I slammed it on the table. His jaw clenched, but he didn't reproach me for my gluttonous libation. I wanted so much to throw the alcohol in his face, but I resisted.

"What happened?" Terrin asked. I looked at him, but realized he was speaking to Rey. "The virus obviously didn't work."

"That's why she is here. I suspect that the virus has either been destroyed by Kit's heightened immune system or..." Rey glanced at me. "It's hibernating."

"Hibernating?" Ayil asked. "What does that mean?"

"It's a state of dormancy."

"I know that," Ayil objected. "What does that mean for Kit?"

"Well..." Rey looked at me like he didn't want to give me any more bad news.

"You're concerned she might still spread the disease," Terrin surmised. "That's why you don't want to release her."

Rey nodded at him. "The Coalition failed to exploit her genetic design when she was sixteen, but I suspect that they have come up with a solution. That's why they are doubling their efforts to apprehend her instead of killing her. I think they may have found a way to switch her on, so to speak."

"So, we'll just have to switch her back off," Ayil surmised.

"Don't worry, we have a contingency plan." Mr. Davis made a slashing motion across his throat.

"Knock it off, Davis," Rayne scolded.

"You don't lay a finger on her!" Ayil stabbed his fork at the man in place of his finger. "Not one fucking finger."

I placed my hand over Ayil's resting hand, trying to subdue his ire. As much as I appreciated his defense, there were too many knives in my back to get picky about the order they came in.

Davis noted the exchange and smiled at me. His once debonair grin now looked lascivious and cruel to me. The fact that I still owed him an open-ended debt made my stomach twist with disgust. Both Rayne and Terrin took interest in our underplayed rivalry, but neither asked the questions that dipped their brows.

Bite Me

Terrin gave me a sidelong glance as I guzzled down my third cocktail. Much to his dismay, I was getting drunk. Or was drunk? I had at least bypassed the tipsy stage.

I wasn't usually much of a drinker, but something about my day—or perhaps my life was requiring less clarity.

Rey had been going on about his theories regarding my immune system. He seemed to think that my DNA contained aberrations that prevented me from getting sick, therefore preventing me from transmitting the potential virus I carried. I had apparently turned into a vaccine factory rather than a carrier. In that sense, I was perhaps closer to what the religious gurus wanted than what the Coalition had intended.

Naturally, I had gotten off the professor's train after the second cocktail.

"That's ridiculous," Ayil contributed. "Of course she can get sick. You've been sick, haven't you, Kit?"

I looked at Ayil and opened my mouth to declare as much, but I was having trouble finding a memory of illness. The sniffles sure, but no pox, no measles, no laryngitis, and no influenza. The only sickness I ever got was homesickness—sick of being home, that is. I shrugged and let out a burp instead of an actual answer.

Ayil stared at me incredulously. "That's impossible."

"Not for her. She is a fountain of potential cures." Rey raised a glass to me and I raised mine. There was only a swallow left in the bottom, but I drank it down under the guise of an unspoken toast and got up for more.

I moved to the bar and grabbed a bottle of whatever was making my drink taste so good. Before I could pour it in, Terrin's hand wrapped around it and pulled it away. He set it back on the cart and leaned in to whisper. "You've had enough to drink." He grabbed the seltzer bottle and poured water into my glass.

Any desire I had for being taken care of or protected by him evaporated in the heat of my anger. I tossed the seltzer he had poured me into his face. He took the assault in stride, only grinding his teeth as the liquid dribbled down his face.

I shifted closer to him, putting my face in his—or at least under his. "Haven't you been listening, Terrin? I'm not a prophecy anymore. I'm a dirty damn bomb. I think I've earned the right to have a drink." I grabbed the bottle again.

"You have, and you did." Terrin pulled the bottle away again. "You're already slurring your words."

I cocked my head to one side and grabbed the bottle. "It's a drink, Terrin, not a hit of *Silverdust*." I gave it a good tug, but he wouldn't let it go.

Rather than argue with him, I grabbed a random bottle off the cart. He grabbed my glass away from me, thinking that it would keep me from drinking myself into a stupor. I didn't bother grabbing a fresh glass; I started guzzling the liquor directly out of the bottle. Terrin yanked the bottle from me, causing me to spill it down my neck.

"Terrin!" I wiped the liquid from my chin. "Knock it off!" I reached for the bottle again, but he pulled it away. I bumped up against his chest, grasping for the bottle like a spoiled child demanding my lolly. The alluring smell of his cologne drew me in, and I leaned against him feebly. Or perhaps that was the alcohol.

"I'm not going to let you get blackout drunk."

"It's not your job to babysit me anymore. Nobody's paying you." When I looked up at him, I saw he was livid. His chest rose and fell heavily, nostrils flaring. I waited for him to blow, but when he spoke, he was the picture of control. More than I could say for myself.

"Why do you do this? Why do you defy me at every step? All I have ever done is try to protect you."

"Protecting me or the Coalition's weapon."

Terrin's ire shifted into shock. He glanced at the table where everyone was still listening to Rey's lesson. "You believe what Rayne said about me?"

"You didn't even defend yourself."

"I shouldn't have to!" Terrin bellowed so loudly that I flinched away from him. The room went silent and Rayne shifted his seat back, ready to intercede if needed. Terrin's eyes bore into mine. He was mad. Really mad. It was a little frightening from my normally stoic companion.

"It doesn't matter why you did it," I whispered. "Your gattaw pride will let you justify whatever you want, anyway. That way, you never have to take any responsibility for hurting me." Turning on my heel, I walked away. I left the room altogether. I no longer wanted to hear about my genes or the lies people had told me.

My so-called destiny had just gone up in flames and I was choking on the smoke.

I made it to the hall not far from my room before I heard Terrin's long strides coming up behind me. I was about to remark about how I didn't want to fight anymore when his hand grabbed my shoulder. He pulled me back toward him and pushed my head forward with his other hand.

I felt his mouth press against the back of my neck. For a split second, I relished the feel of his lips and tongue pressing against my flesh. His mouth spread wide and secured itself to my neck. His teeth pressed against my skin and he clamped down hard, biting me.

I screamed, partly in pain and partly in shock. I ripped away from his hands and lips alike. Spinning to face him, I cradled the back of my neck. "What the hell, Terrin!" I brought my hand forward to inspect it. I huffed and scoffed my outrage at the blood on my palm and aimed it at my attacker.

Terrin's eyes went wide with the same shock I was feeling. He shook his head vigorously and took a step forward. "Mallory, I didn't mean to—"

Rather than run like my instincts demanded, I came at him and ripped the copper sword from his hip. The movement was so unexpected that I got the tip of the blade into the divot beneath his Adam's apple before he realized what I was doing. He froze the instant he felt the pressure of his own sword against his flesh. He raised his hands up in surrender, all the while staring down at me past his cheeks. His body trembled, though I suspected it had little to do with fear. "Mallory," he whispered.

"You stay the hell away from me!" I screamed at him. For a split second, I thought I might press the sword into his neck. I wanted to cut out his lying voice out. I might have tried if it weren't for the damn scent he was wearing. It was so distracting. Why the hell was he wearing cologne?

"Kit!" Rayne yelled as he came running down the hall to mediate the argument that had now become physical. "What are you doing?" he directed the question at me and my raised sword. Rayne pushed my hand, getting the sword away from Terrin's throat. "Put that down! What's gotten into you?"

"Me?" I realized he had missed Terrin's attack on me. He just thought I was overreacting to Terrin's bossy nature.

"Alright, Terrin, that's enough!" Rayne pushed him back, but he didn't really move. "Kit, put that down!" Rayne scolded me again since I was still holding the weapon at the ready. "Terrin, get out of here!"

Terrin swallowed hard. "I need to speak to Mallory."

"She clearly doesn't want to talk to you right now." Rayne glanced back at me before speaking more quietly to Terrin. "You're still cranked up. You shouldn't even be around her. You know that."

"I would never hurt her," Terrin was answering Rayne, but he was still looking at me.

I opened my mouth to object and point out the bite on the back of my neck.

"Terrin!" Rayne stayed between us, though he was just a minor barrier. "Look at me!" I expected Rayne to pull a knife and threaten him, but he kept his movements slow—even gentle. "We aren't in the pit anymore. You're gonna have to keep a lid on those hormones until they clear out of your system."

"I would never hurt her." This time, Terrin turned his answer to Rayne.

Rayne shook his head. "You can't guarantee that right now, and I can't risk it. I'm only going to say this once." Rayne shifted his hand to the center of Terrin's chest. "You either stay away from her or I will put a blade right into your heart." Rayne tapped his chest with a single finger. Terrin looked down at the spot that Rayne was pointing to. "Don't make me do that."

Terrin took a deep breath, broadening his chest. He looked at me, this time with less anger and more disappointment. He reached around Rayne and grabbed the blade of his sword that I still had partially raised. I could have yanked it back and cut his hand, but I didn't. I released it. Terrin didn't say another word before relinquishing his eye contact with me and leaving the hall.

Rayne turned back to me and brandished a finger at me. "Are you insane?"

"Me?" I defended.

"Yes! You don't pick a fight with a gattaw straight out of the dogfights."

"What are you talking about? What's wrong with him?"

Rayne looked down the hall before answering. "You don't understand what they do to the competitors in the dogfights. Painkillers, steroids, and a shitload of hormones." Rayne shifted closer. "It turns otherwise tame men into feral beasts." As he drew back, his eyes paused on my neck. For a moment, I thought he may have seen signs of blood from the bite, but then I remembered the other marks on my neck. The bruises that had not had time to fade. "You're lucky all you got from him on Miorita was a hickey." I shook my head before he said the words. "He could have raped you."

"He wouldn't do that." I rejected the idea immediately, but I was well aware of Terrin's control of me during that encounter.

"He's not the same man you know, and he won't be for a while. He's been getting dosed for the last few months. It's gonna take a while for everything to get out of his system. You need to stay away from him." Rayne turned to leave, but turned his brandished finger back to me. "I mean it."

"Is that why he smells like that?" I asked.

Rayne narrowed his eyes and shook his head. "What smell?"

I opened my mouth to explain, but just gave up and shook my head. "Never mind."

Rayne headed back down the hall, content with his warnings. I, on the other hand, went to my room to staunch the blood of my newest injury at the hands of Terrin. It wasn't as deep as his first assault, but I suspected it would leave just as much of a scar.

Inferno

D r. Kessler's backstory, the man responsible for my DNA profile, was similar to Reynard's. The Coalition had hired both men for their genius and creativity. The pair of them were not only responsible for the biomechanoids, but a host of weapons that the Coalition had been keeping hidden in their arsenals. They were waiting for a rainy day to pull out their big guns. Unfortunately, that rainy day had not yet arrived since I was no longer a functional biological weapon.

Or maybe I was just a very, very late weapon.

Searching for the answer to that very question was how I found myself traversing the planet known by most people as "Inferno." Of course, its real name was "Domus Diaboli" roughly translated as "the house of the devil." Regardless, both names were an accurate description. The planet was not only as hot as hell, but it was also inhospitable to most life-forms. Or should have been, but where there is technology, there is a way.

"How has he survived here for over a decade?" I asked, sidestepping a puddle of molten lava. My heat-resistant silver suit was regulating my body temperature enough to keep my blood from boiling, but lava was another story. The planet's surface was rife with impromptu fire fountains and even the occasional land flow.

"Left!" Rey announced as he shifted to his left. Davis immediately shifted over. Rayne urged Ayil to move left, and I followed their lead. I glanced back to see if Terrin had heard the order. He was keeping his distance as Rayne had instructed, but that meant an inordinate amount of space between him and the rest of the group. He was even avoiding eye contact with me—shifting his head low whenever I looked at him. Part of me was glad he was taking his assault on me so badly, but another part of me felt sorry for him.

I couldn't imagine the hormonal shift he was enduring because of his cold turkey drug use. PMS had nothing on this transition. Not only was he being more aggressive than usual, he was going through withdrawals. His hands were shaking constantly now, and he seemed to be in a great deal of pain. Rey had offered to give him a regimented dose of painkillers, but he refused. He wanted to get everything out of his body as soon as possible. It was admirable, but nonetheless, hard to watch.

Moments after Terrin moved left with the rest of us, a rift appeared in the ground to our right. Steam shot out of it, making the surrounding air foggy. I ducked away from the heat, pulling my hood a little tighter. The scent of sulfur permeated through my static filter, so I pushed my oxygen hose a little deeper into my nose. The fresh flow of air kept me conscious, while the invisible face shield kept ash and debris from going into my lungs. All necessary components to maintaining one's life while visiting Inferno.

"Kessler lives on an island mountain," Rey hollered back to answer my earlier question. "There are a few floating land masses in this hemisphere that can sustain life for long periods of time. Most of them are occupied by territorial wildlife, but Kessler found one that they don't like."

"There are animals here?" Ayil asked, mirroring my shock at this revelation.

"Only a few species, but yes."

"Why don't they like his island?" I asked.

Rey stopped in his tracks and pointed out to something in the distance beyond the fog. "Too steep."

I moved up next to Rey and followed his gaze. It took me a moment to realize that the tall pillar rock formation in the distance was what he was trying to show me. "Holy shit," I mumbled, looking at the sheer cliff walls that were laughably called a mountain. "There's an elevator, right?" I asked, already dreading the walk to the mountain, let alone the precipitous climb.

"It's an elevator of sorts," Rey said with lacking confidence before moving on.

When we reached the cliff, I realized what Rey meant by his vague description of our ride. The carriage waiting at the bottom was far from the usual elevator for tall buildings. It was more like a human sized dumbwaiter. The more I looked at the simple construction, the more I thought about crow's cages from the olden days.

"Ladies, first," Rey offered cheerfully as he opened the door to the contraption.

"How is that a benefit in this case?" I grumbled and climbed in. I tested the metal bars, but found that with my protective gear, it wasn't too hot to touch.

"This thing is safe, right?" Ayil asked, looking over my confinement with dread.

"Of course!" Rey said with unnecessary enthusiasm. "It's just scary as hell. Have fun." The smile on Rey's face looked sadistic as he pushed the button to raise the device. However, *raise* was not exactly what it did.

Rather than lifting upward where it would bump and snag on the jutting craggy cliffs, the mechanism catapulted in a wide arch, away from the ground, and back toward the top.

I instantly dropped to the bottom of the cage. The g-force of the fast movement pushed me down further until the only thing I could move was my mouth—and that was only to let out a horrified scream.

I felt the world flip and then I was swinging back and forth. An angry creak of metal signaled that the locking clamps were activating. Soon after, the cage stopped moving. I waited a long moment, too scared to move. "You can get out now, Kit," Rey's voice sounded over a speaker near the controls. "Push the return button when you're clear of it."

I slowly stepped out of the cage, unsure of my footing since my head hadn't exactly reached equilibrium. I found the return button and launched the cage back over the cliff.

Moving to the edge of the cliff, I watched the cage slam into place at the bottom. Apparently, getting back down was going to be a bit of a headache—literally.

As I stood there looking over the world below, I felt like the devil looking over the vastness of a fiery underworld. To my surprise, it was beautiful. It was turbulent and ridiculously dangerous, but that was the allure. The violent, random sprays of lava were like the endless fountains on Karthik. The rugged, arid landscape was like Miorita. Even the smoky haze below and light sprinkling of ash reminded me of the rainy planet Pallo.

Each place I visited over the years had its own beauty and memories that were equally dear to me. Memories I never would have had if I hadn't left my home. If I hadn't run away from my obligations. An adventure that was never meant to happen, because I was supposed to be dead.

A spider web of red lightning spread across the sky between the dark clouds of smoke. The rumble that echoed through the atmosphere seemed infinite—only silencing after it was too distant to hear. I tracked the sound of thunder as far as my human ears could follow.

As I turned away from the view, I discovered a man standing on the cliff just a few feet away from me. He was wearing a similar heat gear suit. He stared at me, as shocked to see me as I was to see him.

"Hello, Mallory. I'm Dr. Alvin Kessler." He paused a moment, taking a slow breath. "I'm your creator."

Geppetto

Once we were all at the same altitude, we headed into Kessler's home. If it could be called a home. Built into the cliff summit, the house's shape and space conformed to the rock. At the very least, the environmental controls allowed us to remove our suits and stop sweating—mostly.

We found Dr. Kessler in a laboratory just off the foyer, hunched over a short table, pipetting tiny drops of liquid into test tubes. He was not what I had in mind when I thought about mad scientists. He wasn't the scrawny nerd that nervously moved about his laboratory while he talked to imaginary friends. Kessler had the look of a lumberjack. His burly structure had ample muscles and included a bushy, graying beard. Though he wore dark-rimmed rectangular spectacles, that was the only part of him that appeared to be intellectually superior.

Reynard tried to speak to him, but Kessler gruffly objected, as if speaking to a dog rather than a person. Regardless of the demeaning undertone, Rey just smirked and folded his hands across his belly, and waited patiently.

Davis immediately headed to the nearest computer and started hooking up his many devices to Kessler's tech. I wasn't sure if he was just charging his equipment or actually exchanging information. Given the intelligence on both sides of this armistice, I wondered who was benefiting the most from the transaction.

Meanwhile, Ayil began exploring the area. I got the sense he was searching for weapons, just in case this meeting went down a dangerous path. Rayne took a seat on one of the many stools around the workspace and leaned on the counter.

When Kessler finished his work—and after he had placed his tray of tubes in the refrigerator—he finally looked up. "It's good to see you, Rey." His voice bellowed, though I was sure he wasn't trying to yell. He was just a big man with a big voice.

Kessler came around the counter and opened his arms to hug his friend. Though Rey seemed more than willing to take part in the embrace, Kessler stopped short of touching him. His eyes had landed on me and he veered off like a dog distracted by a squirrel.

Again, Rey didn't seem annoyed by his friend's lack of decorum, just amused. He retracted his rejected arms and moved to my side. "May I introduce—"

"Yes, we met briefly outside." Kessler took in a breath, looking me over more thoroughly now that I was no longer covered by heat gear. I felt exposed under his intense scrutiny. I spent so much of my life being examined. It had ironically left me feeling invisible. Being face to face with the man supposedly responsible for my existence was only exacerbating those emotions.

I glanced at Rayne to get his take on this inspection. He just rolled his eyes, as if this was going to be one of those many occasions that I should just go with the flow.

"I'm sorry I couldn't greet you all outside," Kessler said to Rey. "My project has very specific timing."

"Of course. I wouldn't dream of interrupting."

"Thank you for bringing her to me." Kessler's eyes flickered over me with more than scientific interest. At first glance, I might have interpreted it as sexual interest, but the awe in his gaze was not desire. Dr. Kessler was looking at me with paternal pride. A designation that was not only reserved for another man, but completely undeserved. "She's all grown up." Kessler raised his hand to touch my face, and I stepped back. He seemed to enjoy this reaction and turned to Rey.

"Tell me about it," Rey agreed. "She was only three when I left."

"I'm not a test tube, Dr. Kessler. My cooperation with this endeavor is solely in the interest of protection. I'm not here to further your research or to feed your ego."

Kessler's awe of me seemed to wane. He let out a grunting acknowledgment. "I'll need some samples from her. The usual blood, saliva, and urine."

"What exactly are you looking for, Dr. Kessler?" Terrin asked from somewhere near the door. I noted he was even making it a point to stand where I couldn't see him. It reminded me of when I was sixteen and I demanded that he stay in the shadows as punishment for his domineering behavior. Though I knew I was justified in my anger, it still felt wrong to have him sequestered in this way.

"I'm looking for the virus she was infected with just before her sixteenth birthday. The virus that I designed to destroy a nation and disrupt the balance of two governments. To be more specific, I'm looking for evidence of antibodies. The mechanisms by which the virus was destroyed."

"And what will you do with that evidence?" Terrin asked.

Kessler frowned. "What are you asking? What is he asking?" Kessler turned to Rey.

"He's asking if you're going to use Kit to recreate your deadly virus," Ayil said, putting it more bluntly.

Kessler looked over all the faces in the room before landing on mine. "You are my greatest achievement and my gravest sin. I have no intention of duplicating my assignment, but as I'm sure Dr. Baloch explained to you, the virus may be hiding in your system—lying dormant. If that is the case, then I must destroy the virus."

"The virus, not Kit," Ayil clarified.

Dr. Kessler glanced at him, but returned a hardened gaze on me. "I will do everything in my power to protect the world from what I have created."

I got the sense that Terrin had shifted behind me, because Rayne jumped up from his seat just as Kessler threw a worried look over my shoulder.

"I do not wish to harm you, Mallory, but you must understand." He turned his explanation to me. "I didn't create you to spread the common cold. I developed you to house a virus more deadly than any seen in the entire history of humanity. You..." Kessler looked at Rey and he nodded, as if granting permission to the thought forming in his mind. "Perhaps if you understood what it does, you would be more willing to cooperate with my efforts. Come with me." Kessler looked around the room again. "All of you."

Pestilence

Kessler directed us into a room off his lab. It was in such a state of disorganization that I nearly tripped on a pile of clothes at the door. I righted myself and weaved through a maze of stacked boxes.

Much like the lab, Kessler had piles of papers and gadgets littering the shelves and surfaces in the room. I noticed a small cot tucked into the corner, piled high with tangled blankets. Something about the lonesome accommodations made me cringe.

"Here." Kessler waved me over to his desk. He flipped open a small laptop and searched the glossary for a specific file. When he found it, he clicked it open and pulled a chair out from beneath the desk. "Sit," he instructed.

I sat down in front of the screen and watched a video showing a patient in a cloth gown. The young man looked gaunt and slightly dirty. The patient asked the man in a lab coat near him when he would get his payment. Dr. Kessler—a much younger version than the one before me—told him he would receive his money following the trial.

As I watched, my mind dragged a few vague memories out of the shadows of my subconscious. I realized that Dr. Kessler had been among the scientists who regularly poked and prodded me as a child. In fact, he had been the lead poker.

Kessler injected his patient with a yellow substance. I can only assume it was the legendary virus. Only slightly less legendary than the vessel meant to deliver it. Kessler verbally cited the date and time for the camera, after which he shut it off.

When the image came back on, we were in a new location, Kessler reported the time to be 24 hours after the initial injection. He gave the patients stats—which meant nothing to me, but then the camera refocused on the patient, whose health had clearly declined.

Secured behind glass, the young man hammered his fists on it, demanding a doctor. A bought of coughing followed his lamentations. The final expulsion resulted in a spray of blood on the window. He stared at it in shock, then yelled even louder for help.

The image went blank and after another moment, Kessler reported new stats. The display showed the patient crying and leaning on the glass. He looked pale, but his eyes were bright yellow and bloodshot. He begged for a doctor and complained of chest pain.

By the 36-hour mark, the patient was no longer standing. He was lying in his bed, moaning and wheezing. The camera focused in closer on his sunken eyelids, revealing the pus and blood dripping from them. His eyes had either dissolved or deflated.

I didn't have a chance to turn away before the man vomited up nearly a gallon of blood and god knows what. I covered my mouth and turned away from the screen. Terrin and Ayil stared on with disgusted and horrified looks on their faces. Rey looked hardened with shame. Davis and Rayne stood in the doorway, watching with disinterest, as if they were already familiar with the footage.

"I'll stop it there," Kessler said mercifully and turned the video off.

"What's happening to him?" I asked.

"His soft tissues are liquefying. It's a slow, painful process, but in the end, the organs simply fall apart."

"That's awful. You designed it to do that."

"I wouldn't say that was my specific intention, but that was the result. My only saving grace is that the brain is mostly degraded before the internal organs become liquefied. In the end, there is no pain."

"Just in the beginning, then." I couldn't help pointing it out. Up to this point, the idea of being a viral assassin had traumatized me, but now seeing what I could have done to my mother... I was furious. There was no comparing this violation to anything I had ever experienced. This man had used his mind to create something so horrible and then manipulated my genes so that I could carry it to its intended target.

I stood from my chair and faced Kessler. Though he was twice or three times my size, I balled up my fist and threw it at his jaw. I chucked his chin. It was enough to volley his head to one side, but not nearly hard enough to drop him or even make him stumble. I instantly regretted the violence since my hand had not yet healed from my previous attempts to be a boxer. Despite the pain, I refused to diminish my threat by rubbing my knuckles.

Kessler held his head low for a moment before returning his gaze to me. "Can I assume that you will cooperate with my tests now?" he asked, indifferent to my anger.

I was certain that there was a special place in hell reserved for Dr. Kessler, but as the carrier of his sins, I had to share in the burden of sequestering the virus. If I didn't, that reservation might as well be for two.

I huffed out the last of my anger and nodded. "Yes."

Needles

Kessler ushered everyone out of his lab so he could "concentrate." He got everyone except Terrin out the door with an insistent tone. Kessler noted that Terrin was not making the slightest attempt to move and glanced at me. I wasn't sure that I had any authority over him, but I nodded, giving him permission to leave.

He locked eyes with me for the first time in days and shook his head, denying my request. "I'm not leaving you alone with a man who is capable of plotting the destruction of an empire with a little girl."

Kessler's face scrunched in disapproval, but when Terrin turned his determined gaze on him, the doctor resigned himself to having a chaperon. "Fine, but stay out of my way. And don't touch anything."

I watched Kessler meander around the room collecting needles, needles—and god help me—more needles. I occasionally glanced at Terrin, searching for something that was almost never there. Why did I keep looking for it?

Kessler instructed me to lie back, and I did. I compulsively slammed my head against the metal twice to distract myself from the upcoming pain. Kessler gave me a questioning look, but I ignored his concerns.

After a thousand punctures, I should have been used to the clinical invasion of doctors and scientists. But it was hard to put on a brave face knowing that I was a weapon. I was no longer an emissary of medical miracles, advancing humanity with my genetic potential. Knowing that I was an unwilling accomplice to an apocalyptic plague was making me antsy.

Not to mention the last time someone placed me on a table for a medical procedure, a group of thugs tried to rape me.

Before I realized he had moved, Terrin's hand landed on my shoulder. In an instant, I felt at ease. I reached up and touched the back of his hand. I gave him a look that I hope conveyed my gratitude.

"How was it supposed to work?" I asked as Kessler connected me to several monitors—heart rate, blood pressure, oxygen.. He grunted his confusion, but didn't stop working. He scribbled down my oxygen readings on what looked like a scrap piece of paper. I assumed he would input it properly later. "The military aspect," I continued. "I come home. I infect my mother. She dies. What then?"

Kessler shifted around the makeshift exam table, which I had just realized was also his dining table. The dried food stuck to it was bothering me more than the impending needles. Assuming that it was food. Hopefully, it was food.

"The plan was to let Brahama be devastated by the sickness," Kessler answered with clinical indifference. "We projected that it would only take 14 percent mortality to cripple them. Mass panic would set in. If the sickness didn't spread to the nearest planets, we would seed them ourselves. Once the rest of the empire witnessed what they had to look forward to, then the Coalition would swoop in and offer assistance. Naturally, they would use the collective intelligence of their R&D department to come up with a cure. A cure that they had already developed, of course. That is how the control would begin. Wielding their medical help like a set of shackles instead of a wand. A carefully played chess game leading to a monetary entanglement. The empire would be forced to pay for their lives with money and loyalty."

"You were going to bring the empire to its knees with a cure?"

"There is little room left for pride when one is trying to save their life?" Kessler grabbed my arm and cleaned the skin in the crook of my elbow.

"Wouldn't they suspect that the Coalition brought the sickness?"

"No doubt, but after 14 percent of the population is dead, it doesn't matter anymore. You'll beg for mercy from a murderer, just as you would beg for help from a savior."

I hissed in pain, unprepared for the long needle going into my arm. Terrin tensed, ready to attack Kessler, but I gripped his hand, distracting him from *his* anxiety. He glanced down at the contact and wrapped his fingers around mine.

"What made you change your mind?" Terrin asked, returning his attention to the doctor. Kessler once again grunted his query so he could remain focused on his task. "Reynard left the Coalition because he saw the err in his ways," Terrin pointed out. "What about you? What made you flee?"

Kessler withdrew his needle and looked up at Terrin. He didn't seem to like the question. Especially since

Terrin had already questioned his morality regarding his work. "Designing and splicing DNA for high immunity resistance was like a puzzle. I just needed to put it together and make the picture." Kessler looked at me—pride written all over his face. "Which I achieved. Too well, as it turned out."

"You must have been very proud."

Kessler put down his needle and moved around the table to approach Terrin. It was unusual seeing an unarmed human willing to face off with a gattaw. He nodded down at Terrin's short sword. "There is pride in battle. Honor and achievement for besting one's opponent. There is satisfaction in winning." Kessler shifted away from Terrin as if he suddenly remembered that he had work to do. "War, on the other hand, is an exercise in progressive stupidity." He grabbed the needle full of my blood and moved around the lab bench to dispense it into his many test tubes. "In my time with the Coalition, I was revered. They paid me well and gave me anything I wanted or needed. I didn't require much stimulation beyond my work, but I did get the impression that nothing was out of bounds to request." Kessler looked at Terrin from beneath his brow, driving home his point.

"When my work on the disease began, it was just another puzzle. I don't know why I was so ignorant. I would like to make the excuse that my mind works differently than others, but the truth is I was so focused on achieving a goal that I never even considered what I was actually doing. A more indulgent man could at least blame his greed for blinding him, but I had none of that. My eyes were wide open. I just wasn't looking around." Kessler looked toward his bedroom, where we had watched the video of his virus in action.

"My first successful trial looked very different from the numbers on a screen. That man was no one to me—a vagrant as insignificant to me as any stranger. And yet his face has haunted my nightmares for over a decade." Kessler paused, lost in the moment.

"When a man raises his sword in battle, it should at the very least represent his pride." Kessler shook his head. "There was no pride in that form of battle."

Since Kessler seemed to be done with me for the moment, I moved from the table to the edge of his lab bench. "Is that when you left?" I asked.

Kessler shook his head. "My success was followed by an increase in wage and the accolades I received were endless. It was as if everyone was trying to distract me from my thoughts. It was shortly after that first trial when I tried to leave the facility. We weren't a planetary based project. The laboratory was a vessel that could maintain anonymity by circling unpopulated planets. Places nobody cared about."

"I had always been aware that my work was meant to remain confidential, but it had never occurred to me that I would eventually become a component of that secret. When they denied my leave and refused me access to a shuttle, the gild fell from my cage. All the money—the culinary delights, fine wines, and prostitutes—were no longer perks of the job, as they suggested. They were bribes meant to pacify me. I was a prisoner, not an employee."

Kessler's agitation increased with every word. He moved around the room, preparing his equipment gruffly and slamming a few cabinet doors. "It was then that I saw the entire picture. I stopped concentrating on the battle and the war came into focus." Kessler raised his hand as if showing us the billboard in his imagination. "I saw the ignorance of men trying to hold the most power, the most money—and for what!" Kessler turned back to us, his eyes wide and irritated. "We are human beings. We eat, sleep, procreate, and if we are lucky, we can achieve all of that with some measure of happiness. Those who derive happiness from pain are no longer members of the human race! They are parasites, feeding off others for glory and distinction!"

I couldn't have agreed more, but I didn't dare interrupt his rampage. This was no longer a conversation, anyway. This was a decade's worth of therapy sessions crammed into one small room.

Kessler prepared a slide with my blood and fed it into one of his many machines. While it loaded, he stared at the floor. "It was too late to stop the attack, anyway. The virus was created." He looked up at me. "You were created. Stopping it meant killing a little girl." Kessler looked at Terrin. "Maybe a stronger man would have the stomach for that, but I'm afraid I was not willing to add to my nightly penance."

"I sought freedom with the only man I thought could help me. Reynard was the only person to escape the Coalition, so I petitioned him for help. The Coalition was less than pleased to have a second scientist go AWOL, so they hunted me relentlessly. At first, I thought they wanted to detain me—retrieve my intellect—but it soon became obvious that killing me was an acceptable alternative. At least if I was dead, I couldn't use my knowledge against them."

I nodded, thinking that this story sounded familiar. What the Coalition couldn't contain, they would kill.

"For my safety and his, Reynard built me this hideaway. I've been living here ever since. Steering clear of the Coalition and protecting the universe from my ambition."

I looked around the lab again—noting the slightly disorganized appearance. I thought about the room with the small cot and I realized why it had bothered me so much. This was my future. This was the end result of running from the Coalition year after year after year.

The only way that I could save myself and my friends was to be holed up on a nearly uninhabitable planet. For a moment, I imagined a lifestyle of solitude, canned food, and stale air. It was a prison, just the same as any I had known, but one of my own design. A sacrifice for the sake of survival—both for me and those around me.

I suddenly felt claustrophobic. The air in the room felt thicker than before. The residual smell of sulfur was cloying. My decisions had always weighed on me, but recently they had begun to break me. "What would have happened if I had stayed? What if I hadn't run away like you?" I asked, bracing myself for the torture that usually comes with the truth.

Kessler looked up and opened his mouth, but it was Rey who answered. "You would have been killed." I turned to find Rey just coming into the room. He didn't have an ounce of sympathy on his face. This was still just the business of *the better good*. "Make no mistake, Kit. I wasn't lying when I said I have been monitoring you for a very long time. If it weren't for Rayne's run in with Princess Helana, you two would have had a very different introduction."

"What?"

"No." Terrin stiffened beside me.

"Oh, yes. She was next on his list. Kessler may have had qualms about killing little girls, but I didn't."

"Rayne was going to kill me?" I asked.

"Yes, but when that fell through, we decided—"

"You're a hateful bastard, you know that?"

"What?" Rey shrugged, indifferent to the truth that he was sharing.

Rather than explain the concept of emotions to him, I stormed out.

"Why would you tell her that?" I heard Terrin ask before the door closed behind me. I looked around the small foyer, searching for another room. The only other room besides the bathroom was the sitting room. The others were in there waiting patiently for Kessler to finish with me. I took one look at Rayne and knew that I couldn't stand looking at him.

I slipped on my heat gear, drawing everyone's attention.

"Kit, where are you going?" Rayne asked, coming into the room. "What's wrong?" Terrin came out of the lab behind me and Rayne gave him an unwarranted glare, as if he had caused my unrest. Not this time, anyway.

"I need some air," I answered as I put my oxygen mask into place.

"I'll come with you." Rayne moved toward his things, but Terrin reached out his arm to stop him. The action caused Rayne to reach for one of his many knives.

"Ayil," Terrin called behind him into the sitting room. Ayil came out, looking over the situation. "Go with Mallory."

"Why?" Ayil asked, even though he was already heading over to the rack to grab his gear.

"Because she needs the company of someone who isn't going to disappoint her." Terrin lowered his arm and returned to the lab.

Rayne looked thoroughly confused. "Kit." He moved again, but this time, Ayil raised a hand to dismiss him.

"I got it." Ayil pulled his gear off the hook and nodded back to the room they had just been in. "Just go babysit your friend."

Rayne finally relinquished his desire to interfere and headed back into the sitting room. Ayil turned to me as he slipped on his coveralls and mask. "What was that all about?"

"Rey put me on a hit list when I was thirteen. Guess who my assassin was meant to be?"

My hopes for camaraderie dissolved as Ayil's sputtered laughter sprinkled me with spittle. "I'm sorry," he apologized even as his laughter doubled him over. "That's not funny at all."

"And yet you're laughing," I said snidely, even though I was finding some humor in his reaction.

"But it's just so poetic, Kit." Ayil stood up and rested his hands on my shoulders. "You have the absolute worst taste in men." I finally saw the source of his amusement and gave into the irony of my love life.

Immune

After twenty minutes of sitting outside watching the land masses beneath us break and shift like a floating puzzle, Ayil and I headed back inside to join the others. Though we hadn't really done much talking, he had made me feel better.

When I entered the lab, everyone glanced in my direction. Rayne seemed to be perturbed that I hadn't let him speak with me, but I no longer cared what his temperament was. I caught Terrin's eye and mouthed, "thank you," to him. He bowed his head slightly and turned his attention back to Kessler.

"I was just telling everyone that you are no longer carrying the virus," Kessler said. "Your antibodies have done their job and there are no signs of any active viruses in your system." He pointed vaguely at the screen in front of him.

I shuffled over and looked over the data being revealed on his computer via lists and bar graphs. Ayil joined me, peering at the screen with the same feigned interest as me. "If she isn't carrying the virus, why does the Coalition want her back so bad."

"That's what we don't know," Rey said. "In the past I've had spies to feed me information, but unfortunately, Chancellor Agate has sussed them all out."

"It's possible that he has created a new virus off my old work," Kessler said. "I wasn't the only member of his staff doing viral work."

"No, I destroyed your work before I took you out," Rey said.

"Not all of it," Kessler admitted. When Rey gave him a questioning look, Kessler grabbed a handful of paper notes off his counter and lifted it for him to see.

"Oh, you didn't?" Rey chastised him.

"The paper trail I left behind could be enough for someone to manipulate the existing virus or possibly create a new one."

"Even so, I'm obviously useless as a carrier. Why wouldn't they just keep trying to kill me?"

"Because they can't duplicate you," Kessler said proudly. "No doubt they tried with your sister, but they didn't have the right recipe. You are one of a kind." Kessler pulled his screen closer and slid the image over to a list of big words I neither understood nor cared to pronounce. "The key to your gene sequencing was immunity. Humans have five major types of white blood cells. They are designed to fight off viruses, bacterium, parasites." Kessler poked his finger toward the list. "You have eight."

I nodded, trying to follow along. "And that means?"

"It means that you have a secondary defense against disease. White cells are designed to attack foreign material in the body. Once they find it, they multiply and attack. Your body works the same way. The only difference is, it has three additional white cell types that adapt their defenses so fast that you are cured before you get outward symptoms. That's why the virus I created had to be so devastating. It had to be something that even your immune system couldn't surmount."

"But I never got sick," I said.

"No." Kessler smiled—once again looking at me with that paternal pride that I didn't feel like he had the right to project. "Because something happened that I never even anticipated." Kessler moved his screen again, showing an even longer list of big words. "This happened."

"What's that?" I asked, baiting him, even though he didn't require it since the subject was keeping him exhilarated.

"Enzymes. The human body has 1300 different types of enzymes that assist with its functions. You have nearly 2000. Some of which don't even exist in other humanoids." Kessler seemed excited about this news, so I gave him my best contented smile in place of a pat on the head.

"Are you saying that you created Mallory using animal DNA." Terrin moved closer to examine the list on Kessler's screen.

"Oh yes, I used eighty different humanoid and animal species to create her."

"What!" I screeched, nearly ready to punch the next person who gave me bad news. "I'm a flippin' Frankenstein monster!"

"I think a chimera would be a more accurate term," Kessler corrected.

"Shouldn't she have flippers or tusks or something?" Ayil asked as he looked me over for evidence of something abnormal. When his eyes probed to the areas that were hidden to him by clothes, I gave him a not so gentle elbow in his side.

"Not at all. I only spliced in aspects of the bodily functions. The focus of my project was immunity. I took aspects from the golden star tunicate for anti-cancer benefits, the alligator contributed anti-bacterial benefits, and the shark for a natural immunity to viruses. You were created to—"

"Stop saying created like you molded me out of mud. I was born! I have parents!"

Kessler pinched his lips back and nodded penitently. "Yes, of course, I'm not meaning to suggest that I... It's just..." Kessler flustered, so he looked at Rey.

"You have to understand, Kit," Rey said. "You were born to be a vessel for disease. The Coalition lied and told everyone that you were a superior human being with unfounded genetic potential. However, somewhere between Kessler meddling in God's territory and your birth, you made the lie a truth."

I looked back at Kessler and he smiled at me. "You were designed to be a weapon, but you were born—for all intents and purposes—a superior human being with unfounded genetic potential."

I swallowed hard, feeling the pressure of those words being laid back on my shoulders. They had never truly fit before, and now they didn't even feel good. I didn't want to be superior. I didn't want to be special or miraculous. I just wanted to be free.

But that would never happen.

The fate of my future was staring me right in the face. Lab rat or recluse.

Before I could decide which future looked bleaker, an alarm sounded and the lights in the room dimmed. "What's that?" I asked.

Kessler flipped to a new screen, then looked at Rey. "They've found us."

Descend

"We don't have time, doctor!" Rayne dragged Dr. Kessler out of his laboratory before he tried to grab every scrap of paper.

"Come on," Davis threw my heat gear at me. I dressed in record time and followed him outside. "Thirteen minutes—max!" Davis reported to Rey once we were outside.

"What's happening in thirteen minutes?" Ayil asked.

"Thirteen minutes until the battlerunner that just entered the atmosphere is within range to level this entire mountain top."

"Looks like we're taking the backdoor," Rey said calmly and disappeared behind a boulder next to the entrance.

Davis motioned for us to follow. When I rounded the boulder, I saw a larger cage than the one I had arrived in. At least we wouldn't be going down one at a time. Rey climbed into the cage and strapped himself in. Davis pushed Ayil against the wall and strapped a belt across his chest for him. I glared at him when he gave me the same rough treatment, but he just winked at me.

Davis checked his device again and lifted his hand to his earpiece. "Hey Turner, you want to get your ass moving so we aren't turned to ash." Davis listened to his retort and laughed. "Only if you can catch me."

Less than a minute later, Terrin arrived with Kessler. Davis strapped Terrin in while Kessler latched himself in.

"How long?" Rayne arrived with a pile of boxes in his arms, which he passed off to Davis.

"What the fuck is this?" he asked.

Rayne shrugged. "He apparently can't live without it."

Davis rolled his eyes and stuffed the boxes into a metal chest connected to the side of the cage. Rayne strapped himself in while Davis closed the cage. He checked his device and cussed. He strapped himself in and waited.

I looked from him to Rey to Rayne, searching for the reason behind his delay. Both men seemed to be just as impatient as me, but neither demanded that Davis hurry things along. A moment later, a loud explosion signaled the eruption of a lava fountain somewhere below us. The heavy blobs of lava would have been unavoidable, and definitely fatal.

Davis glanced between his thermal detector and the ground below. His foot tapped with urgency that his legs could not facilitate. At some precise moment or temperature unknown to me, Davis slammed his fist into the release button beside him. The cage lowered slowly and everyone seemed to take a relieved breath.

A loud rumble sounded to my left, and I saw something barreling into the atmosphere. It impacted a moment later, shaking our elevator. Another impact destroyed the rock face beside us, showering us with debris.

"I thought we had time," Rayne yelled at Davis.

"We did. They're shooting off the cuff," Davis yelled back.

"Well, they're doing a damn good job."

Another missile hit the top of the mountain, snapping one of our tethers. A corner of the cage shifted down and the metal cable coiled on top of the cage. When the pulley landed, the cage rattled and a warbling *ping* was our only warning before the second support broke and we dropped.

For a moment, I thought we were dead, but the two remaining lines caught us. However, we were sideways and swinging erratically along the rock face.

Gravel and dirt rained down on us as the attack continued above us. Large rocks banged against the cage, clanging the metal and sending vibrations through to my bones. I reached out for Ayil. He found my hand and squeezed it as tightly as I squeezed his.

We crashed into an overhang, knocking loose the third cable. We shifted downward again. Something squawked above us and the fourth cable snapped. I screamed as we careened down. The metal cage hit only a few moments later, jolting us, but not killing us.

Everyone scrambled to get out of their belts. I did the same, but I couldn't move my arm. Somehow, I had gotten it stuck between the bars separating my compartment from Ayil's. I used my other hand to unstrap my buckle and repositioned to pull my arm out, but my shoulder became an issue.

"What's wrong?" Ayil asked.

"I'm stuck," I explained and laughed. "Just my luck. Go ahead, I'll catch up."

"Come on, you two!" Rayne yelled at us from the cage door. Rey, Kessler, Davis, and Terrin were already outside, waiting for us. The impacts above continued to remind me that the battlerunner's accuracy was increasing. "Now!"

"She's stuck!" Ayil yelled back.

"Then get her unstuck!" Rayne returned and assisted me in a forceful tug. Despite his efforts, he came to the same result as I had. My shoulder was being braced between two bent bars. With some effort, I should have been able to yank myself free, but pulling was only resulting in a painful pressure on my forearm. If my elbow were a few inches lower, it wouldn't have been an issue. "Help me pull on this bar."

Ayil and Rayne grabbed onto the bar, holding my shoulder in place. I found a spot to push on it as well. I knew I only needed an inch or two. Our combined efforts resulted in absolutely nothing. After another moment of examination, Rayne held up a finger to me and headed out of the cage to Terrin. He motioned back to me and using several hand gestures to explain my predicament.

Terrin frowned at him and shook his head. Rayne motioned out to the horizon and up to the mountaintop, shattering above us. He pointed to me and shrugged. Terrin nodded and followed Rayne back into the cage.

"Ayil, let's go." Rayne wrapped his arm around his shoulder. "Terrin will get her out. We need to move."

Ayil shrugged him off, but Rayne pushed him along. He looked back at me, confused, but didn't argue.

Terrin looked over my tangled arm and shook his head. "Must you always be difficult?" he teased, but there was no humor in his eyes.

I swallowed hard as Terrin tested the strength of the bars. He was strong, but I suspected the cage could withstand almost anything. If it hadn't been for the final impact, I might have been fine. Perhaps there were rules about keeping your hands inside your compartment, but of course there was no time for a safety lesson.

He looked at the others and back at me. His jaw tensed before he spoke. "I'm afraid we don't have time to cut you out." My heart pounded at the thought of being left behind, but I knew he wouldn't just leave me. He had a plan, but the look on his face told me it was best if I didn't know what it was. He grabbed onto my forearm on either side of the bar. "Please forgive me," he whispered.

Terrin gripped me tight, and his mouth opened in a snarl. He let out of growl that exceeded the vocal range of humans and then... he pushed.

The explosions above were not enough to drown out the horrifying crack next to me. It was as if a branch had snapped right next to my ear. But it wasn't a branch. It was my bone—bones.

The dizzying pain alerted me that something was wrong, but it was the view of my forearm bent around the bar confining me that drove the howl from my throat. Something was poking from my sleeve, having punctured through the fabric. Blood seeped into the yellow cloth. I instantly felt sick and my head swirled.

I yelped as Terrin manipulated my arm out of the binding metal once and for all. The heat that had surrounded me since landing on this planet now prickled my skin from an internal source. I pulled at my heat gear, trying to get it off.

Terrin batted down my hands. He was saying something. I couldn't hear him over the boom above us. Before I could look up, he swept me off my feet and carried me away. Rocks fell behind us, bouncing off the cage we had just left. The boulder that arrived moments after our departure did not bounce. It crushed the metal cage beneath its massive weight, leaving nothing recognizable beneath it.

Rayne came out of nowhere with Ayil. They both had the same expression of horrified concern on their faces. Terrin set me down, and I felt the pain of my broken arm shoot through my body like it was breaking again. I cried out and tried to tuck my broken limb against my chest. Ayil and Rayne used the belts on their heat gear to make me a quick sling.

As soon as my arm was secure, hands pressed on my back urging me to run. Every step jogged my body and made me wince with the pain. My previous state of heat had somehow turned to cold and I couldn't tell if I was shaking or actually shivering.

Weapon fire and explosions continued to fill my ears, along with the rumble of lava spews and the scraping rock of the planet's transformative ground. I couldn't hear the directions being called out by Rey, so I watched for a shift in his movements instead.

Terrin was ahead of me, jogging slower than necessary in order to stay close to me, even though our escape was stretching into a longer and longer line. Rayne was in the middle, near Ayil. He glanced back several times to make sure I was still on track.

Then he slid to a skidding stop and twisted around. He looked at Terrin and screamed something at him. He darted an angry finger at something behind us. Terrin's head whipped around to look at what he saw. Just like Rayne, he skidded to an immediate stop.

The expression of shock on his face was enough to make me increase my pace. I didn't have to, nor did I want to, know what had put that much fear onto the face of a gattaw.

Even as I sped toward Terrin and Rayne, they reversed direction and came running back to me. Terrin drew his short sword as Rayne pulled out a pair of knives.

A shadow fell over me that stretched across the ground at least ten feet in each direction. The scream that should have been coming from my mouth was coming from behind me.

Terrin and Rayne leaped at the encroaching hunter. Feral expressions marred both their faces.

Something grabbed me from behind, latching onto my clothes, and dragging me up. For a split second, it lifted me off the ground, raising me toward who knows what.

As fast as I was up, I was down again, being propelled forward by my momentum as well as whatever the hell was behind me. I skidded and rolled, bouncing across the rocky terrain. When I finally stopped, I was in so much pain that I considered not taking another breath so I could pass out and not feel anything.

I spotted the finale of the battle taking place behind me. Rayne and Terrin were attacking the largest raptor I had ever seen in my life. With a wingspan of at least thirty feet, the bird certainly would have been capable of carrying me away for his lunch. Instead, it was fighting off two blades and a sword.

The raptor's darting beak was its shield and its weapon. Terrin couldn't get near the body without being head-butted or bit. Rayne had the same problem. Even with his second knife for sneak attacks, the bird's heavy layered feathers were making it impossible to cut deep enough to draw blood. Eventually, the bird let out a piercing shriek and flew away—no doubt in search of a less troublesome food source.

Terrin and Rayne caught their breath before meeting up with the rest of the group. When their eyes started darting around, I waved my location to them. Rayne jogged over, but Davis yelled after him. Rayne stopped and waited for him to give him a direction to go, but Davis just frowned at his screen.

The ground cracked in front of Rayne, making him backpedal away from the heat. Even several feet in, I had to get to my feet and move away. When I looked back, there was a heated discussion taking place. Both Rey and Davis were explaining the data on their devices to Rayne.

I looked around for a clear path, but the new split had intersected with other ravines, separating me from the others for the foreseeable distance.

Rayne frantically tapped on Rey's device and pointed downstream. He looked at me and pointed in no uncertain terms in the direction I was to go. He smacked his finger to his wrist, making it clear that we had little time.

Damn it. Time to run.

RACE

I ran along the lava stream, keeping my eye on Rayne as he ran on the other side. I was panting, nearly ready to pass out from heat exhaustion and the pain from my broken arm bumping against me with every footfall. It was all I could do to remain focused on breathing and moving.

Rayne was gritting his teeth and glancing at me. He was gaining distance from me, but I couldn't stop myself from slowing down. Holes and trenches pitted my side of the ground. I nearly twisted my ankle between two rocks, but I managed to somewhat gracefully stumble out of the trap.

Rayne pointed ahead of us. I looked ahead and saw my path of escape. A short land bridge remained between two elevated sections of ground. But not for long. The edges had already crumbled from the molten flow pressing against it. If even a trickle of the lava spilled over it, I wouldn't be able to cross it for fear of death-degree burns.

Rayne saw the same shifting that I did and picked up his pace. I wished I could say I had increased my speed as well, but I was already operating on the last of my adrenaline rush. My body couldn't offer any more speed. Not even with several dangers adding up in my rearview mirror.

Nevertheless, I continued to run, hoping at least that the rate of consumption would decrease instead of increase.

It didn't.

The crumbling edge of the bridge ate bigger and bigger chunks out of the land above it until there was only a sliver left. It seemed to pause then. Rayne yelled at me to go over and with less than thirty feet to go, I could have made it, but I wouldn't have survived it.

I could hear him scream at me when I slowed to a stop. Then he saw what I had predicted. The bridge shifted. While the middle had stopped disintegrating, the edges were still being eaten away. The small landmass broke from the banks and floated down the lava river. A moment later, it went under. I watched it go, thankful that I hadn't tried to cross it. If I had, I would have gone under with it. Unfortunately, that left Rayne and the shuttle on one side of an impassable lava flow, and me on the other. I didn't know how long this river was, nor did I have a thermal detector to track the safety of my movements.

I was as good as dead.

I knew it, and so did Rayne. He stared at me from behind a veil of steam and warbling heat. He was panting and sweating from his run. Worry and frustration contorted his face. I wanted to put on a good face, but I didn't have the energy to pretend I wasn't afraid. Hell was about to swallow me whole and there was nothing anyone could do to stop it.

The others arrived late, clustering along the river's edge. They looked over at me with forlorn expressions.

Terrin was the last to arrive, but he didn't slow to a stop to gawk. Instead, his strides lengthened and his speed increased. He passed the others and snagged the thermal detector out of Davis's grasp on his way by.

I caught his eye as he turned toward the river. I shook my head vigorously, but my pleading face did nothing to detour him. He ran headlong toward the river of lava. Rayne saw his approach and ran to interrupt his suicidal jump, but Terrin barreled through him.

"Nooooo!" I screamed as Terrin vaulted across the molten rock flow.

The distance was easy for him. Less than ten feet separated the two land masses. But that wasn't where the danger lay. Even a few seconds of exposure to the radiating heat near and above the river was too much for his heat gear to withstand.

Terrin landed and tumbled to a stop near me. I ran to him, waving off the steam rising from his clothing. I rolled him over to check for signs of life. He moaned slightly and blinked up at me.

He raised his hand, revealing the present he had brought me—the thermal detector. I was as good as dead without it. Since chucking it across the extreme heat would have damaged the sensors, Terrin used himself as a human shield in order to get it to me.

"Kit!" Rayne's voice came over the device.

I took the multi-function device and found the correct setting to communicate with him. "I'm here."

"How is he?"

I looked at Terrin's sizzling body. The answer was obvious, but wasn't willing to think about it at the moment. I had already faced Terrin's death twice—what was one more time? "We'll need to get him back to the ship as soon as possible."

"Alright, we're going to get to the shuttle and then come back for you." I didn't respond. "Did you hear me? I'm going to come back for you, Kit."

"I know you will." I smile thinly, knowing that he believed what he was saying, even if I didn't.

"The thermal radar has a tracker. Keep it with you no matter what, so we can find you."

"Okay."

Rey and Mr. Davis ushered Kessler and Ayil toward the shuttle. Ayil gave me a longing look, which I returned.

"Kit." Rayne was lingering at the river, not quite ready to leave me. "The land can change in a matter of seconds. If you need to move fast..." He trailed off. I didn't respond, but I looked down at Terrin. He was unconscious now, and I wasn't sure if he was going to wake back up or if he would even want to. "Kit, I need you to be here when I come back. No matter what you have to do. I want you to be here. Do you understand?"

I nodded. "I understand." Satisfied with his pep talk, Rayne jogged to catch up with the others. As soon as they were specs on the horizon, I slumped down next to Terrin and closed my eyes to rest.

Total Drag

"Now, I'm not saying I don't appreciate your company," I said to Terrin's limp body. He hadn't revived since he passed out three hours earlier. "But I think the least you could do..." I grunted as I tugged his body another foot. "...is ask, before you decide to stop by." I checked my thermal detector. We were clear of the first two lava springs I had detected, but the ground was becoming increasingly unstable. I could only see one relatively safe space for us to wait for our rescue, and it was still a quarter mile away. Dragging Terrin the entire way was the only option, but it didn't mean that I was enjoying it.

"I mean, sure, I like you. Hell, I may still be in love with you, but that doesn't mean I can stop everything I'm doing to spend time with you." I paused for yet another break. My broken arm hurt like hell, but the exertion of heavy lifting was helping me forget about it. "Maybe next time you can call first."

"I'll be sure to do that," Terrin mumbled.

I froze, afraid that I had only imagined him speaking back to me, and simultaneously wondering exactly when he had woken up. "Terrin?" I shifted to look at his half-lidded eyes. "Oh, thank god!" I bent down, pressing my forehead to his.

"Not dead yet, huh?" He glanced down at his blackened suit.

"Nope." I surveyed the charred material as well. "I think maybe your suit is stronger than Rey thought. We'll get you fixed up as soon as possible. I called for a ride but they got caught up in a fight with the battlerunner."

"How long was I out?"

I shrugged. "Maybe an hour," I lied.

Terrin looked around at his surroundings. Not that Inferno offered enough consistency to determine where he was, but he seemed to glean that we had moved. He glanced at my hand gripping his collar and then at the other one clutched to my chest. "How is your arm?"

I looked down at it and grimaced. "I think it's broken," I said gravely.

He gave me the barest of smiles. "It wasn't as clean a break as I would have liked."

"Just be glad it wasn't my leg that got stuck."

Terrin frowned at this suggestion. "I should have just carried you."

"Don't be ridiculous." I stood up and repositioned my hand on his clothing. "It makes no sense for one person to exert twice the effort and go half as fast." I pulled on him, moving him an astonishing six inches.

"Then why are you doing it for me now?"

"Because I am assuming that walking on two deeply burned legs will be far more painful than this broken arm."

Terrin pulled his leg up as if he might just try to get himself upright. The gasp that I heard from him made a shiver run through my body. I resisted the urge to breakdown and bawl right there.

"Whoa, whoa, whoa." I leaned down and spoke close to his ear. "Just relax, okay? I've got this."

He took in a breath and put his leg down. "At least let me read the sensor."

I pulled the device from my pocket and handed it to him. He took it and shifted the image in and out. "Where are we headed?"

"That island of solid ground a quarter mile in."

"Are you sure that's wise?" he asked.

"It's my only option. I can't move fast, and there are lava spits popping up all over the place. We must have hit rush hour on the lava flow."

"You mean you can't move fast with me in tow." He looked back at me with a stern expression on his face. I knew what his argument was going to be. "Mallory—"

"We're going to the island and that's final."

He looked over at the determination on my face. Short of swatting away my hand, he had no way of stopping me. He nodded and turned his attention back to the monitor in his hand. "You may want to veer to your right. It looks like there is a hot spot starting toward the second sun."

I pinched the fabric of his suit and tugged him along, angling away from the smaller sun that was setting on the horizon. With only one sun left to go, it wouldn't be long before we lost the light. It didn't much matter except that hot environments usually fostered nocturnal wildlife. And I didn't know enough about this planet to be comfortable with the surprises that the night had in store for us. Between my bleeding arm and Terrin's nearly fricasseed legs, we probably smelled like a barbecue wafting in on the summer breeze.

GONE

"How much longer?" I asked Ayil the moment his transmission came through.

"We..." His voice trailed off. "We had to leave the atmosphere."

I glanced at Terrin, watching the interest in his eyes fade. Despite my cheerful depiction of his injuries being a simple matter of skin grafts, he knew better. The fact that he was still alive was only by the grace of God and his heritage—and possibly his own stubbornness.

As soon as we reached the island and settled into the crag of a cliff that almost counted as a cave, he commented that the pain had stopped. I was certain that he was saying it to make me feel better, but I knew as well as he did what it meant. The nerve endings in his legs were dying because the burns were so deep. The heat had effectively cauterized his legs, cooked the muscles, cut off the blood flow, and now they were dying.

His lower body had sufficiently compartmentalized to keep him alive, but the situation was the equivalent of a massive weight pinching his body in half. It was only a matter of time before his upper body realized it was late to the grave.

The thought had been swirling in the back of my head, but with my history of lucky survivals, I was hoping to save him. Even now, the only miracle I could hope for was saving his life. His legs were well past the rescue stage.

"What do you mean, you had to leave?" I pushed away from the rock wall that Terrin and I were leaning against and headed out of the cave to view the last of the second sun disappearing behind the horizon. The cresting rays of light bloomed from the orb like a rainbow of orange against the teal skyline. The deeper it sunk, the better I could see the dark rings around it. As I understood it, the darkness was still a mystery to even the most seasoned explorers. It was effectively a gaseous smoke cloud that was neither flammable, nor subject to the gravity of the sun's massive weight. For thousands of years, something kept it in stasis, preventing it from approaching or receding.

It was trapped.

Safe, but... stuck.

"We are trying to lure the battlerunner away. The longer we stayed to fight, the more obvious it became that we were waiting for something. So, we left."

"Are they following?"

"Sort of," Ayil said.

"Sort of?"

"They sent about a dozen jetships after us, but the battlerunner is still circling the atmosphere."

"They're checking for survivors," I surmised.

"Yeah, I guess. Rey said that detection is unlikely. Between the planet's heat and the distance, sensors will be useless, but..."

"What?"

"They're searching audio channels for communications."

"They're listening?"

"Yeah, so we can't stay on long and I probably won't be able to contact you for quite some time."

As I looked out over the land of fire and ash, my eye caught on a rock. I hadn't remembered seeing it before. Not that I could trust the scenery on this ever-changing planet. But it was in a rather random spot by itself, so it stood out as odd.

"I don't suppose you have an ETA in mind."

Ayil paused. "I'm counting every second, Kit." He took a breath. "How is he?"

I glanced back at Terrin tucked into the eve of the cliff. His right hand was trembling, and he was panting, but he was still awake. "He's fine," I said dimly.

There was a long pause. "And you?"

I looked back out at the landscape. There were now three rocks that I hadn't seen before and no signs of a lava spring. I chuckled into the radio. "I've never felt better."

Yet another long pause. "Kit, I..."

I watched one of the "rocks" in front of me shift into a flat doom-shaped creature with legs. A turtle of sorts... with claws... and fangs. The bulbous head turned to me. It licked the air and hissed, signaling to the others to unfurl.

"I have to go now, Ayil. If I don't get another chance to say this—"

"Kit, don't," he whispered.

"You need to know that..." I clenched my jaw, fighting my emotions off so I could speak. "I wouldn't take any of it back. Not one minute. Not if it meant never meeting you."

"See, I told you, I was your number one," Ayil teased, but the humor in his voice was strained, like he was holding his breath. "Don't give up, Kit."

"Oh, I'm not giving up, Ayil. I'm just growing up, I think." Sniffling back my tears, I moved away from the three snarling gray carnivorous turtles crawling toward me. "I love you," I whispered and clicked off the radio before he could say it back.

I dropped the device next to Terrin and leaned down to draw his short sword. In his groggy state, he grabbed the blade, causing me to cut him. "Just for a second," I told him, but he was barely conscious, let alone comprehending my words. I tugged on the sword, but he was pinching too tightly for me to get it away from him.

Rather than attempting to wrestle it away from him, I leaned down and kissed his lips. He revived just enough to kiss me back. Our face shields hummed as their energy mingled right along with our mouths. When I felt his hand touching my cheek, I drew back.

He looked at me, confused. When he saw the sword, he looked concerned, but there was nothing he could do to stop me or help me. When I reached the opening, his eyes dipped to the floor and his head sagged.

I turned to face my enemies. Three foaming mouths with darting purple tongues and enough body armor to make me wish I had an ax instead of a sword.

Meanwhile, I was a one-armed competitor with little to no swordplay training. This was going to be a bloody death. One that I didn't relish.

The three creatures turned out to only be the size of large dogs, but their movements were sly. It only took a moment for them to surround me. I shifted left and right, waiting for the attack to begin. I swung my sword at an approaching mouth, cutting a purple tongue right off.

Another lunged at me, but I jumped clear. The third took his turn and spit on me. The sharp sting alarmed me, but I didn't have time to check. All three of them charged me. Their waddling armadillo-like movements were not the frightening image of death that kept me awake at night, but their descending fangs made me retreat.

They increased speed, walking on chubby, stilted limbs. I ran, but my leg went numb, and I became unbalanced. I fell, doing my best not to land on my arm. After inspecting my non-functioning leg, I found three barbs sticking out of my thigh. I yanked them out and stared at the bloody tips. Poison?

I already knew how this would go. Paralysis, followed by three surprisingly lethal hunters eating me... while I was still alive. There was something terrifying about that prospect. Even if the paralysis prevented me from feeling it, I just couldn't fathom watching an animal eat me. Listening to their mouths smack as they chewed me. The crunch of my bone.

I yelled out a war cry that should have come from Terrin or Rayne. My good leg pushed while I used the sword like a pickax to climb a horizontal mountain. I couldn't help but think that Rey's booby-trapped ship had prepared me for this day. Prior to meeting him, I might have let my compromised mobility slow me down, but now it only forced me to push harder.

The creatures hissed at me and slowed their approach. I retreated further, reaching a patch of steaming rocks. As enthusiastic as they were about my tasty flesh, the creatures abruptly stopped. They were not willing to follow me into the heat. Especially since it was one of very few dependable indicators of a lava fountain.

My suit beeped, alerting me to its internal temperature. I was reaching maximum limits. If I didn't get cooled down, I would start cooking in my suit. I considered this death as well. It would be quick and almost painless. Certainly a better alternative to being eaten alive.

Still, I continued to crawl.

The paralysis had reached my broken arm, but it was actually a relief, since I was no longer being encumbered by pain. However, dragging half my body was more difficult than I had expected.

Another alarm sounded on the suit. It was a different notification. It was effectively telling me I was right on top of a volcano and that I should probably move.

There was nothing to do now, though. I was already in the middle of a sulfuric steam bath. I had no idea how big this lava tube was. Some were as small as two feet that bubbled up lava like a water spring. Others were big enough to form geysers that in the right conditions would form new mountains and cliffs like the one Kessler had lived on. Those were the apocalyptic type. The type that made this planet truly uninhabitable.

Either of those would be lethal to me, but judging by the number of perforations in the ground and the distance between the steaming jets, I knew it was neither of those. If I remembered the travel brochure correctly, I had just entered a shatter plateau. Because geologists measured them in acres and hectares, I assumed I wouldn't escape it anytime soon.

The shatter plateaus were areas of land that were too fragile to build up the pressure required for fire fountains.

Instead, the rising lava would break the land apart, turning it into fragments. They would then float along like glaciers in the ocean until they melted down to become part of the flow.

Short of hopscotching the clods—which would be lethal, or rowing myself to safety—which was impossible, there was no chance of survival.

Still, I dragged myself onward.

The ground trembled beneath me. The steamy ejections around me increased in strength and heat. I ducked down to protect my face from a waft of steam that was too harsh for my shield to withstand.

Fearing that I had very little time left, I rolled. It was an awkward movement that required the sword to tip me over and my good leg to follow the movement through, but it was easier and faster than crawling.

I heard the ground groan and snap. The angry planet was stretching—cracking the tender dry skin on the surface. The snaps continued, followed by bursts of splattering lava that signaled a fissure opening in the land.

A clap, not unlike a bolt of thunder, echoed against the crags and cliffs in the distance. It coincided with a shutter in the ground beneath. Then everything went quiet. I stopped to take an inventory of my surroundings. Behind me, the land had broken into dozens of floating islands. There were more fragments to my left and right, but somehow I was still safe.

I hoped against hope that I would stay that way, but as the steam cleared, I could see where I was. I looked out at the diminishing aqua sky in the distance. It was a beautiful sight, especially when seen from the edge of the cliff that I was on. I scooted a little further forward to look over the steep pitch at the valley below.

It, too, was as deadly as it was beautiful. Impossible to descend without falling. Once again, I considered this death to being eaten alive, or boiled in my suit. It had a certain appeal.

Since my suit had reached a survivable level, I put off suicide and wait for the lava to cool and harden, so I could return to the cave. Unfortunately, as I watched the *rockbergs* melt, I noticed that my island of safety was getting a little smaller. The last of my hope for escape evaporated as I realized where I was.

Wind erosion or water flows had not created the rough trails of rock lining the cliff wall. A lava flow had caused this aberration.

I was not sitting on the edge of a cliff at all. I was sitting on the edge of a dormant waterfall—a *firefall*. And it was about to wake about.

As soon as the islands melted behind me, the molten rock would overflow and spill out over the cliff. It would be beautiful. Too bad I wouldn't live long enough to see it.

With no room left to retreat, I confronted the possibility that I had run out of luck. Like so many certain-death situations before this, I had just enough time to look at my life and question every decision I had ever made.

The destiny that I had avoided. The fate I had escaped. And the karmic twist that inverted them.

I lay back against the ground, refusing to acknowledge that I may still have to leap from the cliff to hasten my demise. I hated giving up, especially since I knew it meant leaving my friends behind, never seeing my family again, and never meeting my child.

High above, three raptors were circling. They probably planned to feast on my bones after the turtles were done with me, but they too had lost their meal to the lava.

Or had they?

Surely, such a creature could withstand the heat long enough to grab a nibble. How else could they have survived on this awful planet?

I sat up and jammed Terrin's sword into the rip in my suit where my broken bones were poking out. It should have caused me excruciating pain, but it was still numb from the turtle venom. I drew back the blade and found it coated with my blood.

I knew buzzards could smell death from over a mile away. Perhaps these birds could smell my blood from here.

I waved the sword around as if the extension of my arm might be the extra boost necessary to reach them. I watched them circle, seemingly unfazed by my offering.

My suit beeped, and I looked at see what the issue was. The lava was nearly at my feet. My numb leg was completely oblivious to the temperature that was now scalding it.

I pulled my leg back and scooted a little further, but the cliff's edge was not getting any bigger.

"Come on, you stupid vultures!" I yelled up at the birds, practically double dog daring them to come get me.

It wasn't until a shadow fell over me that I realized there were only two birds circling above me. Glancing behind me, I saw the outline of the third raptor blocking the sunset as it flew toward me.

Cursing, I quickly repositioned myself. I tucked my head down low and pulled my arms in, being sure to keep a death grip on Terrin's sword.

The bird's familiar scream pierced the air as a gust of wind pushed in around me. Something hit me in the back and I careened forward, just shy of face-planting into lava. Talons pressed into my rib cage, cracking my back, and making it difficult to breathe. Then the bird lifted me off the ground.

I glanced down at the plateau as the bird circled, gaining distance from the heat. The space I had been sitting on was now inundated with lava. The dam had finally broken, and the waterfall spilled out over the cliff's edge. I was right.

It was beautiful.

I looked up at my ride—no safer with it than the turtles. Once we were high enough, it rested its wings, and we glided back toward the stable island I had just left. I suspected the bird would take me to the nearest stable peak to have its meal. Though I didn't mind the direction we were going, I had no intention of reaching the destination.

As we neared the stable land, I thrust Terrin's sword upward. It slid past the bird's feathers, effortlessly, unencumbered by bones, and buried into the bird's soft underbelly.

The raptor screamed, and this time it was definitely a scream. Its wings flapped frantically, as if it were trying to clutch them against the wound I had created. Instead of dropping me, it grabbed on tighter, puncturing my skin and possibly breaking a rib or two.

We dropped like a rock and landed in a heap against the desert floor. The bird released me on impact and I struggled to crawl out from under her wing.

Before I left it behind, I reached back and retrieved Terrin's sword. The bird screeched and began flopping about. I scrambled away, steering clear of its death throes.

As I cleared the bird's body, I saw the three turtles I had only just escaped, charging at me. I nearly cried in frustration as I doubled my movements, pleading with any god that would listen to spare me the indecency of being eaten alive. As if in answer, a tingle ran through my poisoned leg. Unfortunately, some of the sensation in my arm was also coming back. I didn't dare stop, though. Broken bones were mendable.

When I was nearly to the cave without a slight tug of resistance, I checked to see how close they were. Thankfully, the turtles were no longer in pursuit. They had stopped to feast on the dying bird. It riled and kicked, but they bit into it without mercy. Strangely, they did not devour the flesh as I assumed they would. Rather, they drank from her with vampiric lust.

The bird's lurches slowed, and soon its cries quieted. I turned away, refusing to watch its exsanguination. A death that had almost been mine.

Mercy

I crawled to Terrin and found him awake. He had stopped panting and started shivering. I knew he wasn't cold—not on a planet that considered a 90-degree-day winter. He was going into shock. Soon, he would go into a coma. Then death would follow.

"Where the hell have you been?" he rasped in a scolding voice. "I need to know where you are at all times. Do you understand?" I stared at him, searching for the joke, but he was serious. "You cannot hide from me. I will always find you. Do you hear me?"

The stern look on his face brought back more than a few memories of my childhood. And not necessarily the good ones. "I..." I trailed off, not sure that any answer would satisfy him.

"What are you doing with my sword? That's not a toy."

"I know. I was just borrowing it."

"Give it to me." He reached blindly for it, as if it was a blur to him. I placed it in his hand and he clutched it close to his chest. "No more running away or I'll make sure you have nowhere to run to."

I stared at him, biting my lip. "I won't leave you, Terrin. Never again. I promise."

His eyes shifted to me and he looked confused. "Mallory, I need you to do something for me."

"What's that?" I asked.

"Tell my father I'm sorry." I shook my head. "He wanted so much for me, and I fought him every step of the way. I shamed him." My mouth dropped as I realized Terrin was no longer in his right mind. Or perhaps he was in the right mind, but at the wrong time.

"No, your father is proud of you, Terrin." I took a stuttered breath. "In fact, I don't think you know how much he loves you. How much he would sacrifice for you?"

"That's what people do when they love each other," he whispered. He reached out for my hand and I gave him my good one. "When we get to Brahama, tell your mother that I'm sorry."

"For what?"

"For losing you."

"You didn't lose me. I ran away."

"No, for not taking you back to her." He squeezed my hand. "I could have, but..." Terrin's eyes lolled, and he started to pass out.

"No, Terrin, don't sleep. Why didn't you take me back to my mother?"

His eyes focused on me again. "I watched you, you know?" He shook his head. "It was different when you were with me. For me, you were just a princess. But out there, you were..." Terrin faded.

"I was what?"

He took a breath and refocused on me. "You were a queen... like your mother." I blinked at the comparison.

It was by no means an insult, but it wasn't my preferred describer. "I shouldn't have, but I couldn't help it."

"Shouldn't have what?" I asked.

"I shouldn't have fallen in love with you." I stared blankly at him. "I never understood why."

I frowned. "You never understood why you loved me?"

"No, I knew why I loved you. I just never understood why it was only ever you. You're the only woman I ever loved, besides my mother. And I can't have you. Why is that?"

I swallowed hard and rubbed my thumb along his hand. "I'm sure the romantics would say that our love would burn too hot if we could actually be together."

"Will you stay with me until I go under again?"

I nodded.

"And when I'm under, will you give me a noble death?"

I stared at him, unable to move without disrupting the tears in my eyes.

"I ask this as your friend. I will not make you promise, but you know how important it is to me."

I still didn't move. I was losing my grip on my emotions.

"I know you are still holding onto hope for me, but there is none. The burns cover one third of my body. My legs are already necrotic. I don't want to survive if I have to lose my legs, Mallory," he whispered.

I finally nodded. He watched me a moment before squeezing my hand tight.

I scooted back to lean against the rock beside him. For a long time, we just sat there, literally waiting for Death to arrive.

"I never told you what my father had to say about you, did I?" Terrin finally spoke. He sounded tired, but he was obviously back to his proper timeline.

I chuckled and wiped away a few more tears before returning my hand to his. "Oh, good lord, I can only imagine what he thought of me. The selfish, stubborn human that was trying to dismantle the traditions of the gattaw."

"Mmm, I do recall there was some conversation about that. But that wasn't what I meant."

"Okay, what did he say about me?"

"He said, 'It's too bad she's a human. She would be perfect for you."

I paused, taking in the sentiment. "He said that?"

"Verbatim. He liked you. He liked that you were willing to risk anything to save me."

"Too bad I can't deliver now."

"We all have to take turns being the hero, Mallory. It can't be you all the time."

I shook my head. "You know I'm not good at sharing."

"I know." I glanced at him, checking his pupils for signs of life. I wasn't sure what stage we were in, but I was certain that there was a reason he was no longer gripping my hand. "He told me about how you wanted to leave Miorita. How you lied to do it."

"Yes, I wasn't as cool-headed in those days."

"I guess we both had a raucous youth—defying rules and running from our obligations."

"To be fair, I was just a boy. I wasn't a prince. I think running from royalty is a bit more dissident."

I chuckled. "I think my mother always suspected that I would eventually do it."

"I'm not sure you hid your desire very well by taking pilot lessons and begging for your own ship."

"No, even before that. When I was young, my mother would always tell me the same fairytale. My father would tuck me in with tales of Sleeping Beauty and Snow White."

"And the Frog Prince," Terrin added.

I smiled, but didn't acknowledge the jab. "On the rare occasion that mother would have time for a bedtime story—it was always the same one. The only unhappily ever after one in existence."

"Which one is that?"

"It was an old earth story about a princess who becomes overwhelmed by her duties to the crown. One night, she runs away and pretends to be a commoner in the kingdom. The queen is naturally very angry, so she sends her guards to get her. The princess meets a man who helps her hide and they fall in love. For a time, they are happy, running and hiding, but eventually the princess sees that the guards will never stop looking for her. They will never leave her alone."

"I hope this doesn't end like Romeo and Juliet."

"No," I said solemnly. "The princess realizes the gravity of her mistake and returns to the castle. Returns to do her duty."

"And the man she loves?"

"She leaves him behind. She chooses her destiny over her dreams."

"I'm pretty certain Romeo and Juliet had a better ending."

"This is the part of the story where my mother would say that you can't think with your heart. That's what the brain is for."

"I don't think I've ever heard you quote your mother," he murmured. I glanced at him, noticing that his eyes were closed and his breathing was becoming shallow. It wouldn't be long now.

"I've been thinking about her a lot lately. I always hated the way she made me feel. Like a chess piece in her game. She was always a hard woman to love, but... I'd give anything to be half as stouthearted as her."

Terrin's hand slipped out of mine.

For a moment, I just sat there waiting. I shifted to face him and patted his face to rouse him. When it was clear that he wouldn't revive, I grabbed his sword and held it over his chest, positioning it between the ribs over the heart.

I was about to press it in when I heard a screech behind me. I looked out of the cave and saw the two remaining buzzards just outside of the cave. They were too big to get to me, but that didn't mean they wouldn't eventually try.

In a world of thinking with my brain instead of my heart, the smart thing would be to finish Terrin off as he requested and drag his body to the entrance. The birds would likely take him as an offering and leave me alone.

Logic was ugly sometimes.

Not that the heart had any prettier ideas.

I stared at Terrin, watching his chest rise and fall. He was alive, but not for long. I was alive too, but also not for long. If the birds or turtles didn't finish me off, I would eventually die of dehydration. It wouldn't take much longer. Not with so much heat and exertion.

Even if Rey returned to save us, his ship lacked the equipment to heal Terrin's injuries. And as he said, he didn't want to live without his legs. There was only one way to truly save them both.

I picked up the thermal detector and thumbed it thoughtfully. I flipped on the radio and punched in the universal coding for a distress signal. I raised the device to my lips and began broadcasting on all frequencies.

"Attention Coalition ship. I wish to negotiate my surrender."

Into the Lion's Den

I walked down the hall of the Coalition ship, arm in arm with two biomechanoid soldiers. Somewhere between them "rescuing" me and the short shuttle ride, I had received about a dozen injections—no doubt for pain and infection. I also had an IV of fluids strapped to my back and a metal healing cuff wrapped around my broken arm. Between the drugs and the relief of not being on the verge of death, I was feeling well enough to face my newest and oldest enemy.

Terrin's body was being wheeled behind us in a medical sleep pod. It was far from the medical attention he needed, but it would be enough to keep his heart pumping until a more thorough examination could be done. The soldiers transporting him veered off into what I assumed was the infirmary while we continued on.

The hallway ended soon after the medical and mechanical sections and dumped us out into the bulk of the ship. Unlike my small craft with twists and turns around every corner, the battlerunner was far less complex. The lower decks served primarily as jetship storage, while the upper decks held other supplies. Between was only a cold, dark, cavernous vacancy. It was as if they had constructed a titanic vessel, but removed all the walls in between.

They achieved most of that space by eliminating the living sections, which on most military vessels took up half the ship. They were unnecessary because there was no one "living" on the ship.

As we entered the hollow space, I took a deep breath through my nasal tubing. A requirement, since the ship provided little to no oxygen for the mechanical riders. Those that required oxygen produced it artificially with built in re-breathers.

I passed by row after row of biomechanoid units. At over two dozen deep on each side and over fifty lines to pass. I estimated that there were at least 2500 units on the floor with me. I didn't even bother looking up into the rafters where the auxiliary units were being stored. I only glimpsed the rows of booted feet waggling as the undead soldiers swayed like marionettes on their designated hooks. That put my new estimate at over 5,000 units.

I ignored the high-sheen black faces I passed, keeping my eyes forward and chin up. Terrin said that I reminded him of my mother and, in this moment, I knew he would say it again. She never showed an ounce of fear in her life, least of all in the company of her enemies. Her backbone seemed to stiffen at even the slightest adversity.

The biomechanoid soldiers stood stock-still as I passed. As creepy as that was, I noticed one in the second row tracking my movements with a slow head turn. After I passed, another one took over on the other side, then a third, and forth, as if they were trading off. Each one taking their turn to monitor my movements.

After my long walk through the gauntlet, I stood in the center of the control room. I noted that the only console was at the head of the room with no buttons or dials. It was just like my interface—a flat black instrument panel. The only exceptions were two slots beside a center basin of sorts. The biomechanoid to my left released me and approached the station. He slid his hands into the smaller slots and placed his face into the indentation. It seemed to be designed for the soldier's face plate.

A moment later, a translucent computer screen image overlaid the viewing window. Codes flickered across the screen, then it went blank. A face projected before of me. The size of the screen made Chancellor Agate's face ten-feet high. His glowing image loomed over me, lighting the otherwise dim room.

He must have seen me as well, because he smiled, but it dimmed as he looked me over. "Hello, Mallory." I hated my name on his lips. I hated that it was the name my father used. Though I was certain I wouldn't prefer Kit any better from him. "Are you alright?"

I glanced down at my sweaty clothes. My shirt was bloody, and my medical attendants had ripped it to fit me with a metal cast. I assumed my face was filthy and the odor permeating from my body wasn't exactly pleasing. "I'm fine, chancellor. I'm more worried about the gattaw I arrived with."

The chancellor's smile returned. "Terrin?" he said, as if pleased with his knowledge. "Yes, as per your demands, he will be given medical assistance. I understand his injuries to be quite severe."

"I was always told the Coalition has the most advanced medical training and technology in the universe. I'm certain you'll be able to help him." It took every ounce of my humility not to make a snide remark about why the Coalition had such expert medical knowledge. There was no room for sarcasm while Terrin's life was hanging in the balance.

Agate looked down for a moment. "I will do my best to live up to your expectations and, in return, I will be getting your full cooperation."

I nodded. "That was the deal."

"That's a very dangerous deal to make, Mallory. I wonder perhaps why now?"

I swallowed hard. "I didn't relish the prospect of being bird food."

"How's your arm?" he asked.

I lifted the cast and knocked on it with my free knuckle. "It's set and the painkillers are working."

"I'm very pleased to hear that. My crew will get things situated for the trip. I apologize in advance for the makeshift accommodations. These ships were not meant for human passengers."

"Not living ones, anyway." I couldn't help adding.

"Why don't you get some rest? We can discuss my expectations after that."

"Chancellor," I said before he could close out his communication. He looked at me, waiting for my next sentence. "I know," I said.

He narrowed his eyes slightly and smiled. "You know?"

I stepped forward, even though the action made me crane my neck upward. The biomechanoid followed behind me, ready to suppress me at a moment's notice, even though there was no one to attack.

"I know everything," I spoke the words slowly. "I know about the virus. I know about your plots to assassinate my mother and cause a holocaust. I know exactly what kind of monster you are." This was not the time to discuss my disappointment in his underhand dealings, but I needed him to know that I was not the same dim-witted little child I was when I left Vigari.

Agate bit his lip as he contemplated my disclosure. He took in a deep, relieved breath and beamed at me—like a child at Christmas. "He's still alive."

My sneer shifted into confusion.

"That's why you were on that wretched planet. Of course, Baloch would have taken you to him."

My enthusiasm for smack talk died instantly. I had just revealed critical information to my enemy. Perhaps I was the same dim-witted child he knew.

"So, they're working together again. This should be tremendously fun." He chuckled. "They didn't kill you, so you must not have any remnants of the virus in your system."

"I don't," I said, pleased that I could at least deny him that. "My immunity to disease seems to be universal."

"Yes, but that does bring up more questions."

"Like what?" I asked.

"Like why you're here. I honestly assumed you were a trap. I thought perhaps they injected you with something new and sent you back to kill us instead."

"I would never willingly participate in genocide—even of my enemies."

Agate scoffed. "That means you really did call me for help. You surrendered yourself to me, endangered yourself further, and for what? To save your former bodyguard? My, how interesting."

"Yeah, I do stupid things for my friends. It's actually one of my most annoying traits."

"That is good to know. Perhaps keeping you cooperative will be easier than I thought."

"I won't spread your virus, Agate. If you think I protect my friends, well, imagine what I will do for my countrymen."

Agate snorted. "You mean the countrymen who you abandoned when you ran away? Please don't embarrass yourself by trying to be a political activist now. Besides, it doesn't matter. While I appreciate being able to tie up loose ends, I don't need you anymore."

My sneer softened into a frown. "What do you mean?"

"I mean, since the last time we spoke, I've found a better option to carry out my *monstrous* plans. If you want to live long enough to see the show, I suggest you do as you promised and behave." Agate clicked off, and the biomechanoid escorted me to my new room in my new home.

Scraps

After a cold shower, I slipped into a medical sleep pod for a twelve-hour nap. Not only did I need the sleep, but it would help speed up my healing process. When I woke, I found a fresh set of clothes lying outside the pod. Or should I say a fresh uniform?

I stared in the mirror at the black leather skin tight suit and wondered if I was compromising my character just by putting it on. Rather than question the morality of fashion, I pulled my hair back into a tight ponytail and slipped Terrin's copper sword into the vacant gun holster on my hip. Since their uniforms were resistant to perforations and cuts, they hadn't taken the weapon away from me.

Even with a sharp, pointy object, I wasn't a threat to them.

I opened the door to my room and found two soldiers standing in wait outside. Neither moved when I stepped into the doorway, but when I moved down the hall, they followed behind me. Not hindering me, just observing. No doubt making sure I didn't screw up their ship. Not that I would even know where to begin. I couldn't even comprehend the pilot interface, let only the mechanics of such an advanced driving system.

I poked my head into a room that I thought might be the infirmary, but it turned out to be a garage for small vehicles—mostly motor bikes and four-wheelers. The shelves lining the back wall contained various items that made little sense for the ship. Shoes, jewelry, wallets, and purses. I skimmed my hand along the shelves, trying to figure out why a ship full of machines would require these items.

I picked up one purse that appealed to me and looked it over. My heart seized when I saw the stain on the back of it and a scorch mark on the handle. I glanced over the remaining items on the shelves. Not all, but many of the items had similar marring.

These were not stocked items. They were just brought on board with the bodies that were purchased and collected by the Coalition. These were the scrap parts of humans—useless to machines. On the bottom shelf, I saw an old communication device. The tech was incompatible with most new technologies, but if I had to guess, it would still work. I leaned down and pocketed the earpiece. My guards either didn't catch the thievery or didn't care.

"Take me to the gattaw," I commanded the one nearest me.

There was a slight pause before he turned and led the way out. I followed him down to the doors leading into the infirmary. The bright room contained medical sleep pods and two massive machines with conveyor belts. I already knew these two systems implanted replacement parts into purchased corpses. That's why the Coalition was so adept at surgical procedures. They frequently rebuilt human bodies, piece by piece.

I peeked in the pods, searching for Terrin. One after another, I found the bodies of soldiers, but not him.

"Where is he?" I asked my guard.

He pointed to a white column behind me. It was one of several in the back of the lab. I stared at it, searching for the trick to opening it. I found a button that appeared to be a light switch and clicked it. The foggy white turned transparent, revealing Terrin.

Or what remained of him.

I gasp and jumped back. I covered my mouth and screamed at his floating, skinless body. His torso was just exposed pink sinew. His legs were even worse. They had cut away the muscles, revealing the bone beneath. He was now just a specimen floating in a jar.

"You bastards!" I screamed and ran back to the tank. I grabbed at the edge of the glass, trying to break it open.

My two guards grabbed me, but I fought against them, kicking and screaming as they dragged me back.

"Let me go!"

"Mallory!" Agate's voice called to me. I looked around and found him standing in the bay with me. I kicked my leg back. My bulls-eye crotch kick warbled the holographic image, but nothing more. "Mallory, settle down."

"You said that you would help him!"

"The injuries were too great—"

"Let him out of there! Let me bury him or burn him, you cannibal."

Agate took a step closer. The guards released me and I stood up to face him. "He isn't dead yet."

I stopped, letting the words sink in. I looked back at the tank and noticed the clear tubes going into Terrin's nose and mouth. There were bubbles shooting up from the base of the machine like an aquarium. The device strapped to his pelvis had several more tubes extending into his other orifices. They had even embedded a large tube into his navel. He was alive, but he still looked like a science experiment to me. "What have you done to him?"

"What have we done?" Agate asked as he moved through me to look at Terrin. "We had to remove 13% of his muscle tissue and 40% of his skin. He was far too damaged for the medical pod, so we had to place him in a reconstruction chamber. I'm still not convinced that we can save his legs."

"You have to," I said, as if my insistence would change medical science. I couldn't and wouldn't subject Terrin to a life that I had promised to protect him from.

"It's going well, so far. The fact that he is a gattaw is helping. His regenerative abilities combined with our stem cell bath will go farther to heal him than transplanted tissue grafts. It just takes longer to heal."

"He'll live though?" I asked, gazing in at the tank. I focused on his face, since it was the least damaged.

"We've placed him in a coma for now. The regrowth will take at least two weeks. When he wakes—if he wakes—we'll know right away if he will get to keep his legs."

I turned to Agate and with every angry fiber of my being suppressed, I said, "Thank you."

He seemed to find this interesting. He shifted to look into the tank. "I'm happy to do it. Terrin was always a loyal employee. At least until he met you." Instead of clicking off the projection, Agate just seemed to walk away into invisibility.

I pressed my hand to the tank and looked at Terrin's slumbering face. He had gone from my Frog Prince to my Sleeping Beauty. Hopefully, it wouldn't take him a decade to wake up.

Stir Crazy

Since my access to the ship was fairly liberal, the next two weeks became more about entertainment than exploration. Though I was taking in my surrounding with the mindset of a magnifying glass, I knew that an escape attempt was impossible. Even if Terrin recovered, there were thousands of soldiers on board this ship and none of them would think twice about snapping my neck and adding me to the Frankenstein constructor in the med lab.

Chancellor Agate paid me a *visit* every day to update me about Terrin's condition. Every day, I asked him why he no longer needed me, as he had said. And every day he said, "All in good time, Mallory."

When I wasn't exercising or sleeping or eating a calorically dense sludge that barely qualified as food, I played with my earpiece, searching for any signal in the universe that could match it. Short of dialing another fifty-year-old device within range, I wouldn't make contact. It was just something to keep my mind entertained.

I was curious if everyone assumed I was dead. If they did, they wouldn't come looking for me. That was sad to me. Not that they wouldn't look for me, but that they would mourn unnecessarily. I wasn't sure why, but I suspected

Ayil would hold out hope for me. He knew I was too stubborn to die. That thought made me smile.

As I mag-skated through the halls of the ship, I picked up speed. There was a slight drop into the main section and I jumped just as I reached it to make my entrance more fun. I whipped around my staged soldiers, one by one, bending my knees and gliding in and out of my makeshift obstacle course with ease. I skidded to a stop at the main controls and swiped my hand across it to check for buttons and switches. Unfortunately, as near as I could tell, the interface required a face and mine wasn't the correct shape. Nor did I compute the same as a machine.

I slid back to my slalom obstacles and moved them back into place. Their obedience amazed me. I got the impression they did very little without specific instruction. So, unless I tried to punch one of them or break into a mechanical room, they wouldn't stop me from doing much.

When I tried to move the last soldier back into line, his hand reached up and gripped my elbow. At first, I thought he might have interpreted my movements wrong and was trying to contain me, but the grip wasn't tight. He was just holding my elbow as if it was the natural reaction to having a woman in front of him.

I knew that the soldier's brain was mush—at least I hoped it was, but still... I wondered if there was a tiny bit of humanity left in there. Hiding between the circuits. Was that possible?

I pressed my hand into his chest. As I did, I felt his thumb shift. He was caressing me with his thumb. I pushed him back into place and his hand released me. I looked around at the other shiny black domes, but none of them were behaving strangely.

I stepped away from the creepy one and skated back to my room. It was going to be at least three more days before Terrin awakened, and it was not a moment too soon. I was going batshit crazy by myself.

Shocking.

I raised Terrin's sword and swung at my makeshift fencing partner. The biomechanoid raised his arm to defend against the attack. The sword bounced off the sturdy titanium arm. I switched angles of attack and he raised his other arm. Back and forth, he predicted my attack and deflected me.

We danced between the lines of soldiers in the main section; me trying to get the upper hand, him just repositioning for the next attack. Thankfully, his programming limited him to monitoring me, otherwise, my newest game would have been lethal. This recreation was as much about relieving stress as it was about getting cardio. Plus, I was testing the boundaries of his restrictions. I figured out yesterday that a forceful forward thrust would provoke him to take my sword away. So, for today, we were just sparring—so to speak.

"I see that you are making use of my soldiers," Chancellor Agate's hologram appeared behind the guard.

I lowered my sword, panting from the exertion of exercising in a low oxygen environment. Thankfully, Agate had increased the flow so I could move about freely without a breathing apparatus, but it was still like walking up a cliff just to get from room to room.

"Good morning, chancellor," I greeted him civilly, even though I was not in the mood for his pompous antics.

"What brings you by so early?" I moved to the guard, holding my water at the ready. I took it from him and popped the top. "I thought we had a lunch date." I guzzled down the water in one long drink.

"I'm afraid I just couldn't wait to see you. I have a surprise for you." He moved to his soldier and, with a simple hand gesture, the biomechanoid returned to his position in line. When Agate noticed another outlier, he threw me a perturbed look when he. "Why is my soldier wearing a smiley face?" he asked, pointing to the two dots and arch I had painted on one soldier's face shield.

I shrugged. "I don't know. I think he just finds something amusing." I crossed my arms, faking my contemplation. "If it bothers you, just ask him to turn around." I stared at Agate, double-daring him to do it.

He waited a long moment, but eventually his curiosity got the better of him. Another quick hand gesture and the soldier turned around. I smirked as Agate read the note I had left for him. It was the equivalent of a bathroom wall slur, but I was pleased to watch his jaw clench with dissatisfaction.

After another long wait, he let out a breathy chuckle and nodded. "I understand."

"I hope so," I said. "I didn't use big words."

He turned a look of admiration on me. "No, I mean, I understand why you have reduced yourself to this level of mockery." He sauntered over to me, giving me a sympathetic look. "You've been put in a position that you have virtually no control over. You have to find ways to rebel. To make yourself feel empowered. This little display, while nettlesome, is completely excusable."

I sucked air between my teeth and grimaced. "Oooh, you might want to check on the others before you forgive my insolence so readily." I tried to maintain my cool indifference, but my mouth broke into a mischievous smile.

Agate frowned and turned to the soldiers. "Company!" The soldiers tensed in unison. "About-face!" The entire division pivoted so their backs were facing us.

Agate gazed over the various attachments on the soldier's backs, as well as the writing that was scribbled next to them. He approached the first line and touched the wallet that was duct taped next to the name Malcolm Kent. He shifted his gaze to a handkerchief I had stuffed into another soldier's back pocket. On its back it read, Trudy Dalton.

Purses, belts, scarves, watches, photo chips, key chains, necklaces, charred grocery lists, and bloody love letters. Fake fingernails and glasses. Barrettes and wigs. Diamond rings and magnetic implants. Next to each attached item was the name of a man or woman that had been used to construct an army of the un-dead.

I stepped up beside Agate and touched a pocket knife that was taped to the back of one of them. "I found a list in the medical database. I thought the soldiers should have names." I turned to him expectantly. "Do you like it?"

"Mallory, I'm very aware of the people's perception of—"

"Why do you cut the breasts off?" I asked.

"What?"

"The women. They have no breasts. Do you do that to make them look like men?"

Agate took a breath and turned to me. "In our experience, people are more likely to cooperate with authority figures if they are male or at least gender neutral."

"Comforting to know that sexism can cross the boundaries of technology."

"Isn't it though?" he said earnestly. "You know, I really wish that you would have saved this for another day."

"Ah, did I ruin your surprise?"

"Not at all, but I'm afraid that what I'm about to show you is going to seem like revenge now. In reality, it's just a very fortunate discovery."

I didn't like the conspiratorial delight on his face. He wanted me to ask what he had discovered, but I didn't want to. I hadn't gotten a pleasant surprise in months—possibly years. I didn't want any more.

Agate looked down and moved his hands over a device that did not appear in his hologram. When he looked up, the room around us was lit with additional holographic images. The extension of the visual forced the image to be grainy and slightly translucent, but I could see that I was now on a different ship. One with brighter walls and smoother surfaces.

"Where are we?" I asked, looking through the glass windows to my left and right. A medical bay, perhaps?

"This is the Coalition's laboratory." He motioned to the image overlapping the soldiers. "It's a Mecca of scientific innovation."

"This is where you held Kessler," I pointed out. "And Captain Baloch."

"Yes, prior to their defection."

"You do have a history of people running away from you. I wonder if it has something to do with you being a fiendish asshole?"

"Enough, Mallory!" Agate scolded. "I've had quite enough of this behavior for one day."

"Sorry, I just react poorly to imperialistic prats."

Agate's lips twitched, and he snapped his fingers. A biomechanoid stepped into the mirage and punched me in the lower back. The concise hit rocked my body with pain and I had no choice but to buckle and wait for the pain to subside. While I kneeled on the floor, I glared at Agate. He shook his head at me, disappointed.

"You haven't changed much, have you?" He moved back to me and crouched down. "You always were a self-important little bitch. I suppose we did that to you. Between the crown and being told that you were the savior of the human race, you were bound to get a pretty big head on your shoulders. I should have hired Terrin sooner. He could have disciplined that arrogance out of you at a young age. Then we wouldn't be in this situation, would we?" He shifted his head to hear me. "Would we?" He looked at the biomechanoid.

"No," I answered, disappointed that it only took a small amount of pain to buy my cooperation.

"Good. Get up." Rather than wait for me to rise, he motioned to the guard, and he lifted me upright. "I still need to show you my surprise. I was going to wait until you arrived to show you in person, but I thought it might be better to break the news this way."

I walked down the hall with the help of the biomechanoid holding my arm. I was really just walking down the line of soldiers in the main bay, but they were now just a blur behind the walls of Agate's lab. Several men in lab coats walked the halls with various digital devices and medical equipment. Though I could see them, they didn't seem to see me, and walked right through me without even glancing at me. I wondered how many men and women they had recruited for this work. Did they know what evils they were creating? Did they understand the devastation their science was creating? Did they even care?

Agate showed me to a door that positioned me at the head of the ship. He stood by it and waited for me to give him a questioning look before speaking. "You've been asking me why I no longer need you. The answer is inside this room."

I frowned at the door, not wanting to go inside. I didn't want to see, but eventually I would need to see the truth that was contributing to Agate's dark plans for the future.

I took a breath and stepped through the hologram.

I arrived in a dimly lit room on the other side. Somewhere from the shadows, the sound of a mechanical suction ebbed and flowed. There was a beeping sound, steady and rhythmic, cutting through the other machine. A long plastic curtain surrounded the instrumentation and a medical sleep pod.

"What is this?" I asked.

"Look a little closer," Agate suggested rather than telling me. He was enjoying this surprise more and more. My fear was taking hold of me, but I stepped forward past the plastic containment barrier. Beyond that was another. I passed through it the same as the first. I got the impression the maze of plastic walls was in place to protect the staff from whatever was at the center.

Visions of a monster lying in wait entered my mind before I settled on a more realistic conclusion. One that I wanted even less than the demons in my dreams or the serpents in my midst.

Somewhere on the other side of the last foggy plastic curtain, an ultraviolet light illuminated the inside of the medical sleep pod. I slipped through the last barrier and stonewalled my heart against the body I saw through the window of the pod. A site as gut-wrenching as Terrin's torn-up body and as heartbreaking as watching his father sacrifice himself in the dogfights.

I recognized her chubby cheeks, blonde hair, and her bulbous, surrogate belly. Beyond that, she looked nothing like the Aresties I knew. Sallow, pockmarked skin covered her swollen arms and legs. Her lustrous hair was dull and broken. Sensors and devices of every kind imaginable were attached to her.

"What have you done to her?" I wanted to scream and beat on Agate's chest until he gave me an answer, but he was only an illusion.

"We didn't do anything to her. We are saving her."

"Saving her?" I could hardly speak the words. They were so wrong. "What is this? Why is she here? How did you..." I trailed off, realizing that the Coalition must have picked her up and taken her to this lab. But for what purpose? "What's happening to her?" I settled on the most pressing question.

"To put it simply, she's sick," Agate said. He stepped through the curtains and joined me next to the pod. "Did you think I wouldn't find out?" he asked. I looked into his determined gaze. "Did you think you could hide this from me?" he asked.

"Why is she sick?" I asked.

Agate looked down at Aresties. "She's sick because of you. I know you thought you were protecting her, but the child—the child you gave her—is killing her."

I felt nauseated.

My stomach twisted and roiled at the sight of my friend in the hands of the Coalition and on the verge of death. As much as the truth hurt, it was the guilt that was weighing my heart down. Everyone I loved was constantly being put in danger because of their connection to me.

This had to be the last straw. The final slap in the face. I wanted to stop the ship and get to the next available sanitarium to get a lobotomy.

"What's happening to her?"

"Aresties was never meant to carry your child."

"Why?"

"Because she doesn't have your antibodies. During the last three months of pregnancy, a fetus must rely on passive immunity. The mother protects the child from bacteria and viruses. When you transferred the baby, it lost access to that."

"Can't Aresties provide the immunity?"

"Sure, if your baby was normal, but it's not. Like all of us, the child's genome is made up of ten percent viral genetic material. Echoes of viruses that have been embedded in our DNA and passed down generation to generation. In most humans, these are effectively junk DNA and can't hurt us, but your child seems to be—how should I put this—cultivating that genetic material."

I frowned at him. "My baby is growing viruses?"

"Oh, yes, it's quite something. Aresties is currently infected with eighteen different viruses. Three of which have not been seen since the dawn of space travel. My geneticists have never seen anything like it. It's as if the child is a virus factory."

I stared down at Aresties' bulbous belly. I wasn't sure I could be angry at my child's behavior this early in its life, but it warranted my disappointment. The baby was continuing my trend of hurting its loved ones.

Or perhaps it was Rayne's killer instinct it had inherited. Our child was turning out to be an assassin. It would claim the title of youngest serial killer before it was out of diapers.

"What's going to happen to them?"

"We've got her in medical stasis. It's slowing down the fetal development, but the baby will survive. Once she gets to the end of her term, we'll perform a C-section." Agate turned to me. "I doubt she will survive the procedure. As it is, she is barely hanging on."

"Don't you have any cures for these diseases?"

"We have all the cures."

"Then cure her, so she can survive the pregnancy."

"There's no guarantee the child will continue to produce these viruses as it develops. It's best to keep everything just as it is."

I narrowed my eyes and took a step away from him. "This is why you don't need me. You..." I looked at Aresties and scoffed. "All the data that Kessler took when he left. You don't need to get it from me, because it's right here. You're using her as a goddamn petri dish to grow your diseases."

"Yes." Agate showed no sign of remorse. "And if things go well, we'll get to use your baby as the weapon that you failed to be." Agate chuckled. "It's ironic, really. Your baby is a plague, and you were the only cure." He took a step forward and bent his head as if to whisper to me. "I guess it's a good thing you're here, then."

I swung the copper short sword at Agate's head, but naturally it sliced right through the illusion. He showed his enjoyment of my display before dissolving the surrounding holograms. When I was alone again—give or take 5,000 biomechanoid drones—I let out a horrific scream that I once again thought belonged to the owner of this sword.

Grateful

I had taken to punching one of the softer biomechanoids in my quarters. It was the only exercise that relieved my boundless guilt. My mother and one-third of the empire were going to die because of my baby, and there was nothing I could do to stop it. I couldn't even get the damn communicator I stole to work, so I couldn't warn anyone about it.

"Mallory?" Terrin's hoarse voice carried over to me from the door.

I froze, not wanting to turn around. Not wanting to see how crippled he was. Not wanting to see what I had stolen from him by not letting him die a noble death.

I turned slowly and looked at him, leaning on the door frame. He was still wet, presumably dumped out of the hydro-pod moments ago. He had wrapped himself in a plastic sheet from one of the exam tables. There were still a few tubes hanging off his shoulders and dragging on the floor behind him, but I was fairly certain he would have ripped out the more invasive ones the moment he awakened.

I swallowed and took a small step toward him. "Terrin?" I whispered and examined his legs. They were clammy and a sickly shade of green that didn't match the rest of him, but they appeared to be intact. "You're—"

He took an unsteady step forward and dropped to the floor. I rushed to him and put myself under his arm to help him back up. "Where are we?" he rasped.

"We're safe. Sort of," I answered evasively. "Are you in pain?" I asked.

"No." He grunted as he rose again. "Just extremely stiff and tired... and wet."

"Come on?" I urged him over to the sleep pod I was no longer using as a bed. He may have been conscious now, but that didn't mean he was ready to be functional. "You need to sleep your sea legs off."

"I just woke up."

"Just for a couple hours," I assured him.

"What happened?" he asked as he climbed into the pod.

I removed a few unnecessary tubes and folded his excess sheet inside with him. "We'll talk when you wake up." I closed the lid, but he grabbed my wrist. He said nothing, but he looked worried, like I was leaving him behind. "I'll be here when you wake up. I promise."

He released my arm and retracted into the pod. I closed the lid and watched him through the window. I pressed my hand to the glass, and he raised his to the inside. In less than a minute, his eyes drooped and his hand slid away from mine. I watched him sleep a while longer, rejoicing in his rising and falling breaths, before returning to my workout.

After a quick cold shower, I sat down in the med lab for a late meal. The dehydrated vegetable medley did not appeal to me, but this ship's design didn't accommodate people with healthy digestive systems, so I was fortunate to have any food. As I crunched on my seaweed bar, I once again tried to activate the ear com I had snagged from the storage room. The device was useless without its twin, but it made me feel better to try.

"They certainly make these uniforms tight."

I was concentrating so hard that I hadn't heard Terrin sneak up on me. I got a second startle when I caught an eyeful of his well-endowed body practically bursting from the black leather biomechanoid uniform I had put out for him.

I practically choked on my bar crumbs and looked away as I coughed. I grabbed a drink of water before attempting to find his eyes beyond the spectacle of his lower half. "They usually castrate the males. There's a machine over there that can get it done if you want to make room." I nodded toward one machine in the back.

Terrin looked at it, a deep crease forming between his eyes as he no doubt contemplated this treatment. When he looked back at me, my lips were desperately trying to burst into a smile. "Very funny," he said, though there was little evidence of humor on his face.

"Don't worry, after a few weeks of eating this crap, you'll lose ten or fifteen pounds. That's how I got mine to loosen up."

Terrin eyed my uniform, which, like his, was beyond snug. "That is loose?" he asked, almost as if the word itself was foreign to him. "I'm sorry I missed the tight version," he mumbled. "May I?" he motioned to the chair—aka plastic storage cube—across from me.

His formality absolutely delighted me, but I couldn't let it go without another sarcastic remark. I hissed through my teeth. "I don't know. I was supposed to meet someone here." I leaned over as if to check the door for my belated party.

"Is there someone else here?" Terrin asked in earnest and whipped his gaze to the door.

I sighed at my ever-failing attempts to add humor to Terrin's life. I pushed the cube out for him with my foot. "No, just me and about 1800 eunuchs."

"You must feel right at home with so many unattainable men," he said as he sat down.

I blinked at him, waiting to see if this was his attempt to return my satire, but he didn't smile. Rather than let myself get drawn into an argument about my questionable taste in men, I continued with the pleasantries. "Shows what you know. One of them lovingly touched my elbow the other day. I think I've got a shot with him."

"Is that the same one you were using as a punching bag?" Terrin grimaced and shifted on his cube. He eventually caved and reached down to adjust himself manually to stop whatever was pinching him in this new position. I tried not to be amused by his fashion difficulties, but there was something adorable about the frustrated pout on his face.

"We can make some alterations if you're too uncomfortable." I slid the hilt of his sword out of the hip holster that was intended for a pistol. He must not have noticed me wearing it when he came in, because his eyes landed on it like a predator.

His gaze shifted to me, flickering over my face. I sensed a certain pride there—or perhaps it was gratitude. He had likely assumed that I had lost it or that the soldiers had confiscated it. After a moment, his head tipped and his eyes narrowed. "What exactly are we altering with that?" His face finally allowed for a slightly teasing smirk.

I chuckled and slid the sword back into place. He watched it go behind the view of the small table. "Do you want it back?" I asked.

He looked at me as if he didn't know why I was asking. "No, I know you'll take care of it. Besides, it looks good on you."

"Do you even remember me taking it?"

Terrin looked down as if trying to recall. He shook his head. "I don't remember much. And what I do remember, I can't differentiate from my dreams. I thought I was going to die. I guess the Coalition had other plans for me. How did they find us?" he asked. It was the question I had been dreading since he woke up.

I sat silent for a moment, considering my options. I could lie, but it would likely come out later and a delay wouldn't make him any happier. "I told them where we were."

The subtle change in his face warned me he was holding back a tidal wave of anger. If he were a normal gattaw, he might have upended the table by now, but a unique set of rules governed him. His calmness was a better indicator of his unrest.

I leaned back and crossed my arms. I kept a watchful eye on him, waiting for him to speak. However, his jaw was so tense, I doubted he could get the words past his teeth.

He stared right back at me with the same patience, waiting for my determination to waffle. Under different circumstances, I might have pleaded for forgiveness or immediately justified my actions. Today, however, on this ship, after the news of my child and a thousand more regrets lining up behind that, I didn't give a shit if Terrin was mad at me for saving him.

He seemed to glean that I was in no mood for a lecture. If he wanted an argument, he would need to be prepared for the fallout that it would bring. He unclenched his jaw and glanced back at the hydro-pods. "Tell me what happened."

"You were dying. Reynard wasn't going to return anytime soon, so I negotiated for our rescue."

"Negotiated?"

"My location and cooperation in exchange for them saving your life."

"I was ready to die."

"I wasn't. I had maybe an hour left before the raptors got to me or I dehydrated."

Terrin looked around at the room. "You could have figured something out."

"I'm sure I could have, but after surviving a trio of hard-bodied predators, narrowly avoiding burning to death, and using a giant predatory bird as a taxi, I thought I deserved a break."

He frowned, as if he wasn't sure if this was another joke. "I know you did this for me."

I stared at him, unwilling to admit that I knew my enemy was the only option for his survival. And that I would make the same choice a thousand times over.

"You shouldn't have—"

"You don't have to thank me, Terrin." I stood up, gaining enough height to lord myself over him properly. "But don't you dare ask me to apologize. I've done far worse to protect you."

His frame stiffened, and he took in a deep breath. This was intolerable for a gattaw—to be scolded by a human, and a weak one at that. Once again, it was only his personal ethics that prevented him from "putting me in my place." However, that didn't stop his expression of anger from morphing into contempt.

As comfortable as I had become with Terrin over the years, it was easy to forget how dangerous it was to bait his anger. Seeing that I was shredding his last nerve, I reached down and shoved my food and water across the table to him. "Eat something. I know you're hungry. When you're ready to talk to me like an equal instead of your underling, I'll be in the main bay."

I moved to storm out, but he caught my wrist as I passed. The grip was not something that I could wrench away from, so I didn't bother trying. I didn't even look at him. Out of the corner of my eye, I could see that he, too, was staring forward, not looking at me.

As the standoff dragged on, my heart raced, and my breathing hastened. I couldn't help thinking about the bite Terrin had given me after my alcohol-infused insurrection. And that Rayne was not around to save me.

All at once, Terrin released me and ate and drink as I had commanded.

I finished storming out—though now it was more of an escape. This was not how I wanted our first conversation to go. I hadn't even told him how happy I was to see him. Or how grateful I was for his sacrifice.

I spent the next twenty minutes pacing the bay. I debated whether I should apologize to Terrin, even though I had already mandated that I wouldn't. I also considered apologizing for my high-handed reprimand, even though

I had every right to make a decision that would save both our lives.

I didn't understand how he could be mad at me for saving him. How was that any different from him risking his life for me? Granted, turning myself over to the Coalition was a bit like handing a nuclear weapon to them, but since they already had a nuclear weapon, it didn't matter. Not that I knew that at the time.

"How long have we been here?" Terrin called over from the entryway to the bay.

I looked back at him, once again startled by his quiet approach. He didn't look angry anymore. Which was good, but since I was still sick to my stomach about our exchange, his stoic demeanor made me want to punch him in the face.

I shrugged. "About a month."

He whistled as he descended the short incline into the cavernous area. "So that's why you're punching the biomechanoids." Terrin strolled along the line of soldiers, making it a point to touch them, as if to check to see if they were awake. Or perhaps he was just curious about what they felt like.

He quickly discovered that a firm push would knock the soldier off his designated position, resulting in an immediate return to his post. It took me several days to learn that you had to instruct them to "halt" after putting them in new positions. And even then, they would return to their posted location after I left the room.

Terrin noticed the soldier with a residual smiley face on his face shield. "That's a long time to be alone."

I nodded, not bothering to count my daily check in with the chancellor as company.

Terrin turned his attention to me, his brow creasing with concern. "Are you okay, Mallory?"

The last of my anger melted away and a month's worth of loneliness, guilt, regret, and fear seeped out of my muscles, making my body sag. "They have Aresties," I blurted out. "They know she's carrying my child." Terrin's gaze faltered as he considered the ramifications of this. He opened his mouth to speak, but I cut him off—since I was quickly losing my capacity to speak. "The baby is turning out to be the viral weapon they always wanted me to be." My lower lip quivered. Terrin moved closer, his face etched with sympathy. "My child will kill Aresties and anyone else it encounters." Terrin's strides lengthened as my voice shook. "They're going to release a plague on the empire, starting with my mother, and I can't even warn her." I broke down the moment Terrin reached me. He pulled me in tight and pressed my head to his chest, stroking my hair as I bawled.

"When is this ever going to be over?" I raged through my sorrow.

"I don't know," Terrin answered honestly. "But we will find a way to stop this." He reached down and lifted my face to look up at him. "We will get off this ship and we will warn her."

I loved hearing the certainty in his voice, and my heart surrendered to the idea of being rescued by him. Unfortunately, as a short-time resident of this ship, I knew we wouldn't escape. We now belonged to the Coalition—as prisoners, slaves, or lab rats.

"I'm sorry for..." I paused, not sure that I could say the words he wanted me to without diminishing my autonomy. "I'm sorry I keep making you angry."

He let out a discontented breath before moving his hand to stroke my face. I thought perhaps he might apologize to me for being overbearing, but he didn't seem to have anything to say about his behavior.

I ignored his lack of reciprocation and nuzzled into his chest. I was grateful that he was alive, even if he was a pain in my ass. I only hoped he felt the same way.

I breathed in what should have been his intoxicating scent, but all I could smell was the artificial smell of his confining suit. I let out a soft, dissatisfied groan.

"What is it?"

"I miss your cologne."

"Cologne?"

"Yeah, that scent you were wearing on Rey's ship."

After a brief pause, Terrin pushed back to look at me. "I don't wear *scents*." He said the word as if it was beneath him to take part in the human custom.

"Oh, I guess it was just your natural smell," I said, rather impressed.

Terrin shook his head. "You've never mentioned that I have a scent before.

"You never have."

Terrin brought his zipper down and exposed his chest. "Do I still have an odor?"

I chuckled. "Well, don't make it sound bad. It's a rather nice smell." I leaned forward, giving his chest a sniff, but I could no longer smell anything beyond his suit. I shook my head.

"What did this scent smell like?"

I strained my brain to find the vocabulary for what I had smelled. "It was earthy and floral, with a hint of..." I closed my eyes, trying to remember what the prevailing aroma was. "It reminded me of your father's stew, actually." I opened my eyes to see what he thought of that and he looked positively disturbed by my description. "Well, I mean, it's not like you smelled like food, but the roots he used…" I cleared my throat, realizing that I wasn't making him feel any better. "It was probably just the drugs."

"The drugs."

"Yeah, all the hormones and steroids they injected you with in the dogfights. Maybe they messed up your glands or something. Do gattaw have pheromones?"

"Yes, but why would you…" Terrin's brow dipped as he looked me over.

"What's wrong? You look mad again." I sighed, disappointed that I had already pissed him off again.

"No. Not at all." He zipped his uniform back up and pulled me toward him, embracing me again.

"Do I have an odor?"

He smiled. "Generally, yes. As all humans do."

I frowned. "I'm guessing it's not floral."

Terrin let out a deep chuckle. Rather than answer, he tugged me in tight and kissed the top of my head. "Come," he ordered and ushered me forward with a firm grip on my shoulder. "I'm still hungry."

Requited

I laid on my bed—aka two exam tables and about six layers of foam lining that I had stolen from the other sleep pods—while Terrin paced my quarters.

"What about access ports?" he asked.

"There's only an incinerator and a jettison tube. The incinerator has no safety switch and—" I yawned through my words. "—the jet tube doesn't do us any good without space suits."

"And you've tried to get to the jetships?" he asked, going over the same information.

"The minute I reach the stairs, they intercept me. The minute I try to open a vent and crawl in, they intercept me. They are watching me 24-7." I motioned to the door where two biomechanoids were just hanging out in the hallway. "I don't even get to shower alone," I mumbled. "Pervy bastards."

"Can you be serious?"

"I am being serious. They watch me pee for crying out loud."

"Mallory, we need to figure this out."

"I know, Terrin!" I sat up in my bed. "Do you think I've been spending my days playing connect the dots with the star charts? I mean, that's not all I've been doing. I've explored every inch of this place and I haven't found a safe way for us to escape. And while I am so glad to have a real live person to talk to—I am exhausted." I slumped back on my mattress. "And I need to sleep."

Terrin frowned and moved to the edge of my bed. "You're right. You should rest." I could see his eyes plotting out something.

"You should rest too."

"I've rested enough."

"You've just had your legs reassembled. You need to sleep." I patted the bed, and he looked down at it like I had offered a chair with a Whoopie cushion on it. "It's the only soft surface in the house. Trust me."

His eyes drifted to the floor. "I think it's best if I sleep elsewhere."

I knew he was probably right, but it still felt like a rejection of me more than the bed. "Whatever." I shook my head and rolled over. "Just turn down the light on your way out."

I cuddled into a cluster of uniforms that I had ripped apart and sewn together again as a blanket. I sensed Terrin was debating his next move. When the light switched off, I closed my eyes, ready for a break from my day. Who knew that Terrin's presence would stress me more than his absence?

I heard the door shut, and I assumed he had left to do his own exploring. However, the sound of a zipper descending alerted me to his proximity. I glanced back and saw him shrugging out of his confining jumpsuit. He slipped it off completely, revealing a pair of rudimentary gray underwear much like my own. The undergarments, like the uniforms, were comprised of stretchable fabric that provided only minimal protection against the suit.

Terrin actually sighed after he tossed his uniform away. I snickered and rolled back over. "It's not that bad."

"Speak for yourself," he said and crawled into bed beside me. There was enough room for both of us, but he scooted up behind me rather than situate himself on his half. I felt his hand on my hip and I jumped in surprise. "Do you mind? I don't want to be gored in the middle of the night when you roll over."

I realized then that he was unbuckling my holster. "Oh, sorry. I usually sleep with it on. It makes me feel safe." I lifted slightly so he could pull the belt from beneath me.

"Well, you don't need it tonight." He leaned over me to place the sword on my makeshift night table. His body pressed against me as he did. "You have me," he whispered before withdrawing.

I felt my heart race as I tried to remember the last time Terrin had been in my bed. Was I just a girl? I wasn't a girl anymore.

Terrin stretched out on the bed, taking up every inch that I wasn't using. "Don't hog it all." I teasingly kicked him.

"Mmm, that's what you get for inviting a gattaw into your bed."

I chuckled. "Is that so?"

"Oh, yes, a bed hog and trouble." I felt him pinch my side, and I shifted away with a squeal.

"I'll give you trouble." I grabbed my pillow—aka stuffed tote bag—and attempted to hit him with it. He intercepted the bag and tucked it behind his head.

"Thank you."

"No, no, no, that was not an offering." I tried to tug it away, but he kept it secure with one hand. I laughed, but it turned into a groan. "Terrin, I need my pillow."

"You wanted me in your bed, so here I am." He patted his chest and invited me into the crook of his arm. I stared at him, suspicious of the invitation. He wasn't usually this playful. I now debated if *I* should sleep somewhere else. "If you're worried about my state of mind, you should know that my treatment has cleaned out all residual drugs and hormones. I'm the same dispassionate man you've always known. So, there will be no more biting." He perked his brow. "Or anything else." Despite his reassurance, his eyes took a leisurely stroll over my body.

Baffled by his contrary behaviors, I let out a sulking sigh and settled in beside him. He wrapped his arm around me and pressed me close. I laid my head against his bare chest. I thought perhaps I could smell his scent again, but it was only for a second.

"Comfy?" he asked.

"Yeah," I said, even though I wasn't at all comfortable. My heart was thumping so hard that I was certain he could hear it. With my breasts pressed against him, I suddenly didn't know how to breathe. And I was no longer the least bit tired. However, I loved his warmth and the feel of his skin under my fingers. I wanted so badly to run my hand along his belly, to feel the surprisingly silky texture, but I suspected it was the skin much lower on his body that was really calling to me and I couldn't risk the temptation.

Instead, I traced my finger along the slight ridge of his sternum. It was not nearly as pronounced as some gattaw, but still different enough to be considered alien. "Is this why the gattaw are so strong?" I asked in a whisper.

He looked down at my finger, tracing the bone. "Among other variations." He brought his hand up and touched my fingers, touching him. I lifted my hand, and he continued to caress my fingers. He pushed his fingers between mine and then drew back to press the tips of my fingers to his. "I'm sorry I frightened you earlier," he said as he tickled my palm.

"It's fine," I murmured, enthralled by his soft touch.

"No. It's not." He dragged his fingers down to my wrist and gently took hold of it before bringing my hand forward to kiss my fingers. "It makes me sick to think that the one thing I can't protect you from is me."

I didn't have a response to that. It applied to so many aspects of our relationship. Never mind that we were biologically incompatible. The real danger in our relationship was that it was in his nature to maintain order. My disobedience had always been a source of contention for us, but it wasn't until recently that he had reverted to physical domination to keep me in line.

The strange thing was, the threat of his strength had always been there. The possibility that he could force me to bend to his will was not new. While the dogfights may have diminished his restraint, it was still his own instincts he was acting upon.

I wasn't afraid that Terrin might try to hurt me again. It was my lack of fear that frightened me. I believed him to be worthy of my trust, but I was extremely biased when it came to him.

Terrin released my hand and pressed it down to his chest with his on top. For a while, I listened to the lullaby of his heartbeat. Just as the Sandman dragged me away, Terrin spoke again.

"Mallory," he said softly, questioning if I was still awake. I mumbled a response. "What did you mean earlier, when you said you had done far worse to protect me?"

My eyes flipped open, and the Sandman fled back into the shadows. I shrugged against his body. "Nothing."

"You said it rather adamantly, like it was something you truly regret."

"It's nothing. I'll tell you later."

He reached over and caressed my cheek. "Tell me now, Mallory." It was an order to be sure, but his voice was soft, almost seductive. It wasn't as easy to defy him when he was being so intimate.

I sighed and pushed away from him. I huddled on the end of the bed to keep my body as far away from him as I could while a spoke. "It's not that big of a deal, but you're going to be mad at me for being so stupid."

"Perhaps I should sit up for this." Terrin shifted himself up to lean against the wall while I revealed the untold story of my greatest humiliation.

"When I was at the dogfights, I needed some information about Dagon. His weaknesses and former injuries. Basically, I wanted to give you an upper hand at winning. Which gave your father an upper hand at winning, I guess. Anyway, Davis had the information, but he wouldn't share it unless I paid him for it. Since I didn't have enough money to bribe him, and my credit stamp was off limits, I had to pay him in another way." I rolled my eyes.

Terrin shifted as if he wanted to leap out of the bed and strangle someone. Since the preferred neck was not present, he moved back into feigned relaxation. "You paid him in sex?"

"No, although, I almost think that would have been better."

"What do you mean?"

"I mean, Mr. Davis is a primo asshole. He made it seem like he wanted sex. He ordered me to take off all my clothes, so I did. When I was buck-naked under the stadium, he asked me to get down on all fours. I waited for him to..." I paused and swallowed back some of the lingering emotions that surrounding his actions. "...get on with it. But he just stood there and laughed. He told me that he had already leaked the information to benefit his own betting. He just wanted to see how much it would take to turn a princess into a whore." I hugged myself into a tight ball, blinking away my unnecessary tears.

"That explains Ayil's demeanor toward him."

"Ayil still thinks I screwed him. I was too embarrassed to correct him. I know it's stupid. I should be glad he didn't touch me, but at least if he were just some horny asshole, then it would have been this secret between the two of us. Now it just feels like a nasty prank."

"Regardless of the lacking sex act, he still defiled you—your character, your honor. Why didn't you tell me about this?"

"Because you would have killed him."

"Yes."

I laughed at the certainty in his voice.

"You were right about me being angry. You shouldn't have sacrificed your body to save me."

"It's just sex—or would have been. Besides, you sacrificed your legs for me."

"There has to be a line that you won't cross for me, Mallory."

"Clearly not." I raised my hands, displaying my predicament.

Terrin shifted forward and crawled across the short expanse of the bed. He kneeled before me, staring me down. I held his gaze, searching for the definition of the sternness on his face. "When you came to visit me in the caves on Miorita..."

I swallowed hard, realizing that he was about to start the grownup conversation I had been putting off since we arrived on Rey's ship. It was probably for the best to do it sooner rather than later. Being alone with him on this ship was turning out to be more arousing than I had expected. Why was the threat of internal bleeding never enough to stifle my stupid hormones?

"There was a point when you... gave up." I narrowed my eyes, not understanding. "You surrendered to me. You were going to let me have you."

I shrugged. "You're too strong. I couldn't get you off."

Terrin shook his head. "Then you bite my lip into your teeth meet. You dig your thumb into my rib cage. You fight me until I come to my senses."

I scoffed. "Are you seriously blaming me for almost getting..."

Terrin nodded. "You can say it."

"No." I moved off the bed.

"Where are you going?"

"I changed my mind. I prefer to sleep alone." I snagged my pillow back from him and headed to the door.

"Mallory, we both know how that could have ended. Rayne was right. I could have raped you."

"It wouldn't have been rape, Terrin!" I screamed at him. He opened his mouth to speak, but I cut him off. "Don't you dare give me the incompatibility speech! I'm sick of being reminded of it! I know I can't have you, but that doesn't stop me from wanting you." I opened the door to leave, but turned back to brandish a finger at him. "And another thing! Stop making jokes about my taste in men. Whether you are willing to admit it or not, you are just as much to blame for fostering my ridiculous crush."

"I have done everything possible not to encourage your feelings for me," he argued.

"Maybe that's the problem!"

"Excuse me."

"I'm alone in this. I know you're in love with me. I know that you want me. And yet, I'm the one being ridiculed for it."

"Ridiculed?"

"Yes, I'm the stupid human who can't keep her emotions in check. Meanwhile, you..." I scoffed. "Well, you either have a far greater control of yourself or..." The anger I was feeling morphed into a profound sadness as I considered the alternative. "Or you just don't love me as much as you claim to."

Satisfied that I had said my piece, I turned to leave. I didn't hear Terrin move. Nor did I comprehend what was happening until I was slingshot back into the room by his grip on my arm. I cringed as he brought me to him, uncertain if he intended to hit me, bite me, or kiss me. Instead, he held me close to him, pressing me as close as my defensive arms would allow him.

"My love may have grown slower than yours, but I assure you it is not lesser." Despite his physical aggression, his voice was soft. "You accuse me of fostering your crush, even when I have stifled every emotion I ever felt for you. If you don't want to be alone in this anymore, Mallory, then I will join you. I will tell you every day how beautiful you are. I will touch you as often and as freely as I truly desire. I will engage you in a way that only a man in love can. Is that what you want? To wallow in my torture and your own? You want me to be in pain with you?"

I considered this and shook my head, appalled. However, the more I thought about it, the more I realized it was true—at least to some extent. "Yes," I whispered as meekly as I could to keep my shame to a minimum.

"Then know it, Mallory." He moved his hands to my face. "I long for you each and every day. And it pains me, beyond measure, that I cannot be with you."

He released me and stepped back. For a long moment, we just stared at each other, the distance between us growing cold. "Take the bed," he commanded more than offered. "I'll sleep in the pod."

I gathered my pillow, which I had dropped to defend myself, and moved back to the bed. Terrin, meanwhile, climbed into the pod, keeping the lid open so it didn't activate unnecessarily. After we were both situated, I considered saying something else. Something that might bring some closure to our fight or make one of us feel better. I battled with my mind for nearly a minute before saying, "Goodnight, Terrin."

"Goodnight, Mallory," he said back.

Checkmate

T hree days had passed. Terrin had awakened, and we still hadn't devised a workable plan for escape. Despite my assurances that I had checked every nook and cranny, Terrin had spent the days exploring the ship. I knew that part of his detailed search was just a way to avoid me.

As heated as our argument had been, the aftermath was ice cold. Apart from crossing paths in the med lab and very limited conversations about mundane details, we hadn't been socializing at all during the day. At night, we slept apart to avoid any discomfort.

I had thought knowing Terrin was feeling the same thing I was would make it easier to be around each other, but I was wrong. We had always had an elephant in the room of our relationship, but now it felt like the elephant had left, leaving behind a gigantic pile of dung. As much as we had avoided the elephant up to this point, neither one of us wanted to deal with the shit he left behind.

While Terrin had spent his time exploring, I had spent the days building a chess set out of computer parts, surplus hardware, and jewelry. It was the ugliest and oddest chess set that I had ever played, but I was desperate for mental stimulation. Something to clear my mind. Not to mention, I was looking for any excuse I could to interact with Terrin without conversation.

He was not the biggest fan of board games, as I had discovered long ago on our first space taxi trip, but I convinced him it was a game of intellect and not a child's source of entertainment. That seemed to pique his interest.

He accepted my invitation to play and endeavored to learn the rules. Unfortunately, he was a fast learner. By the third game, he was beating me well before I could start a strategy.

Terrin stared me down across the board. We were both lounging on the incline leading into the main bay. The chess board was between us on the higher platform. I had been looking at my pieces for a few minutes. "Rook to—" Terrin suggested.

"Don't help me, I can do it."

"Clearly not," he mumbled.

"Don't get smart with me horn-head or I will make you play the dice game."

His eyes widened. "Oh, not that damnable game. I hated that one."

"So did I."

"Then why did we play it so much?"

"Because I liked tormenting you." I pinched my lips back to contain my smirk, but I wasn't hiding any of my delight from him.

"The truth comes out." Terrin narrowed his eyes at me.

"You were a good sport. Especially since you didn't feel well. How long did it take you to get your space legs?"

"I spent the first year hunting you with my head in a toilet."

I laughed rather boisterously at that and Terrin glared at me. "Sorry." I wiped a few joyful tears from my eyes and settled down. I cleared my throat. "I really do feel bad for everything I've put you through."

Terrin shifted and moved my rook where he thought it should go. "I know. As do I." He glanced at the brace on my arm before making his next move. A smart person would have entered a medical sleep pod upon arrival and would have their arm healed by now. But I had wanted to monitor Terrin. Now that he was awake, I just didn't want to miss anything. "You know I didn't know, right?" Terrin asked.

"Know what?" I looked over the board, trying to remember which of my pieces was the queen.

"I didn't know what their ultimate plan for you was." His face wilted with shame. "I think I suspected that they weren't telling me everything, but I didn't question it. I naively thought doing my duty was the most important thing."

I stared at him, shocked that he was apologizing for doing his duty—something I never thought he would do. "I didn't suspect you of being part of their plots." I picked up my knight and moved it before he could move it for me. "I was just too upset that night to think clearly. Too many secrets being revealed all at once. Too much... everything. A girl gets testy when she gets downgraded from superhuman to supervillain."

"You are not the villain."

"No, I'm just the gun he carries." Terrin frowned and returned his attention to the game. "Speaking of too much. Can I ask you something?" Terrin peeked at me from beneath his brow. I sensed he was dreading my question even before he knew what it was. "That night... Why did you bite me?"

His head snapped up, but his eyes went immediately back to the board. He moved his piece without thinking, putting him right in the path of my bishop. "I was angry and not in my right mind. I thought Rayne explained my hypersensitive state."

"He did, but I just... I mean... I get that I pissed you off. I get that you were frustrated with me. I was intentionally needling you, but I would have expected a slap or maybe to get slammed up against a wall. I didn't expect to be bitten." I moved my piece and took down his knight. "Or is biting a common disciplinary action for gattaw?"

"No," Terrin said curtly. "It wasn't discipline. The skin of a female gattaw is not as delicate as that of a human woman. I didn't mean to draw blood. I bit too hard. I misjudged my strength. I'm extremely angry with myself for not being more careful with you."

I nodded, accepting his explanation for drawing blood. However, that still didn't explain the action itself. "So, biting a female gattaw is normal."

"Sometimes, under specific circumstances."

I got the sense that Terrin did not want to tell me something about his reasoning for the action he took against me. Which only made me more curious. "And do you want to share those circumstances with me... the one you bit?"

Terrin huffed and shifted to sit up a little more. "Must we dissect my actions during a hormonal rage? It's not exactly my proudest moment."

I sat up to meet his gaze. I didn't want to start another fight with him, but I also didn't want him to brush me aside. Since I bore the marks of his abuse, I deserved an explanation. "It wasn't exactly mine either, Terrin. I know I was drunk, and I know I was pushing buttons I shouldn't have, but I don't think I deserved to be dehumanized for it."

Terrin's brow dipped deep. "That's not what I was doing."

"Okay, then explain it. The only thing I have to compare it to is a mama cat herding up her kittens. Tell me what the biting was about, so I don't have to feel so debased."

Terrin's eyes widened and then fell. He looked back at the board and made his move before answering. "In gattaw culture, there isn't a marriage contract. Sometimes there is a celebration of love, but that usually takes place on the anniversary of the first child or on another meaningful date for the couple. There are no rings or name exchanges. When a male and female begin mating... a male will bite the back of the female's neck to bruise it. The mark signifies that she is taken."

"Like branding a cow?" I asked dismally.

"No!" Terrin snapped. "It's not meant to be demeaning. It's the equivalent of an engagement ring in your culture. Since females walk behind their mates, the mark is meant to signify that the woman is spoken for. It prevents any confusion. Most females renew their marks regularly as a symbol of love."

"Like polishing a ring?" I asked.

"You asked for honesty. Don't ridicule it when you receive it," Terrin sniped.

"I'm not. I promise." I raised my hands in surrender. "Just a bad joke."

Terrin shifted back down to the board and played another move, even though it was my turn. I looked over the board, trying to concentrate on the game, but I couldn't. "Okay, sorry, sorry. I don't mean to keep badgering you, but I'm still not understanding the precise motivation."

"What do you mean?"

"I mean that you and I were butting heads pretty hard that night. I'm pretty sure you wanted to rip my head off, but instead you gave me an engagement ring."

Terrin's face muddled with a mixture of ire and confusion. "It's not a literal engagement... it's just... I couldn't... I wanted..." He trailed off, frustrated by his inability to explain to me what was probably a simple concept to him.

He stared across the bay at the stars floating by on the viewscreen. "I felt like I was losing you," he finally said. I wanted to ask what he meant, but I just waited until he found the words he wanted. "I told you once that there would always be a part of you that belonged to me. There was a pride in that for me—at the time. That no matter what—no matter what man lay in your bed—a few of your heartstrings would still be tethered to me."

Terrin glanced at me, but I tried to keep my face stoic as to not influence his candor.

"In hindsight, I can see that the part of you I was clinging to was that little girl who blindly worshiped me so long ago. I wanted to keep her so that I could still be adored by her, even if it was just part of a fairytale."

Terrin shifted to face me. "That night I watched you defy me time and time again—baiting me into a fight that I didn't want to have. I couldn't make you listen, and it infuriated my already fragile temperament. All I could think about was that you were no longer mine. You weren't afraid of me at that moment, and you certainly weren't in love with me. I watched you walk away, and I knew that I would never get that little girl back. She would be gone, and I had nothing to offer the woman that was left."

He took in a deep breath. "So, I grabbed you and I bit you as hard as I dared. Because at that moment it was the only thing I could think to do. The only way to hang on to what was mine."

I licked my lips and nodded. It wasn't the explanation I expected, but I supposed it was the one I needed. "I see," I said, because there was nothing else to say.

Terrin continued to stare at me, waiting, I suppose, for a reaction. I didn't have one beyond the stupefied and stunned look on my face. It was my turn to gaze out at the stars through the viewscreen. I thought about how my love for Terrin had changed since I met Rayne. It was true that I no longer revered him like a lovesick teenager, but I considered that a good thing.

I cleared my throat. "I get what you mean about me belonging to you. Like I gave you a piece of myself." I winced at how stupid that sounded in words. "I've been thinking about what you said the other night about me wanting you to be in pain. Maybe your pain is what I want now, but it isn't what has been missing in our relationship." I frowned, unsure if I was just shoveling more shit into our relationship. "The thing is, though, I've never felt like I've had a part of you."

Terrin's brow dipped. "Mallory," he whispered and reached out to grip my hand. "I've been with you every step of the way—even when I wasn't right next to you."

"Exactly," I murmured, more to myself than him. "You've always been right next to me, but you've never been with me. I've had your loyalty, but not your heart."

Terrin pulled his hand from mine, no longer wishing to console me. "And I've always had your heart, but never your loyalty."

Heat rose through my body, fusing rage to my words as I spoke. "I risked everything to get you off Miorita. If that's not loyalty—"

"It's stubbornness," Terrin snapped. "If you had left when I told you to, we wouldn't be in this situation."

"Oh, please, if you really want to backtrack, why don't we go back to my first mistake? Go ahead, Terrin, remind me how all of this is my fault for running away in the first place."

"Don't be dramatic, that's not what I'm saying."

"No, that's exactly what you're saying, because your definition of loyalty is me doing whatever the fuck I'm told!"

"With such a feeble understanding of loyalty, it's no wonder you can't recognize my heart."

"I can't recognize what I have never seen." Terrin looked truly shocked, and I instantly regretted my words, but before I could apologize, he stood up.

He looked down at me. No sign of the heart I might have just broken. "I think you're getting confused between my heart and my cock, Mallory. While I may never give you the ladder, the former has belonged to you for quite some time. Perhaps you didn't recognize it because you were too focused on what I can't offer, instead of what I could."

Terrin walked away, and with every distancing footstep, my anger morphed into shame. Tears bloomed in my eyes as I reached down and moved one of my pieces directly into the path of destruction. "Checkmate," I mumbled on Terrin's behalf.

I maintained my composure for another moment before I hurled the game board and all its pieces at a row of biomechanoids. I curled into a ball on the hard floor and wept for many more reasons than I could focus on.

Sparring Partner

Terrin and I had spent another night in cold company, not discussing the issues that were continuing to bleed into even our most civilized conversations. Despite our limited access to the ship, I hadn't seen him once since I woke. As relieved as I was to avoid another fight, the lack of companionship was making me go stir crazy again. I was seconds away from throwing my feces when he arrived in the main bay.

"You're doing that wrong," he said from the entrance.

I looked back at him, panting from my stress-relieving activity for the day. I knew I wasn't the best swordsman, but given that my sparring partner was a biomechanoid ordered not to harm me, I thought my progress in the battle was going fairly well.

"They don't really fight back anymore, so I have to pretend." I batted the copper short-sword against the soldier's side. He belatedly shifted his iron rod to block me.

"I don't mean your attack. I mean your style."

"I wasn't aware that swordplay required a style."

Terrin moved out of the door and marched over to me in the center of the room. He stopped next to the biomechanoid and took the iron rod from his grip. He shoved the soldier back into his place in line. "Swordplay is for humans."

"I'm pretty sure I've seen plenty of gattaw fighting with swords."

"Yes, but they are strong. You are weak."

"Wow, going straight for the jugular." Terrin slammed the rod against my sword and it dropped to the ground. Before he could get an earful of my ire, he yanked me over to him and pressed the iron rod under my chin. "Understanding your weaknesses is the first step to learning how to fight."

I scoffed and tried to yank my hand away from him. Since he wouldn't release me, I pushed the bar away from my neck instead. "I don't want to learn to fight."

"Nonsense. If you are going to be wearing my sword on your hip, then you should know how to use it to your advantage."

"Then you can have it back." I ducked under the bar and broke his grip on my wrist. I picked up the sword and tossed it to him. He caught it easily. I walked away, just as disinterested in fighting with him physically as vocally.

"How many games did I play with you over the years?" Terrin asked as I reached the entrance. I turned back and saw him balancing the blade on one finger, holding it perfectly parallel with the floor. "By my count, I learned 50 human games. I played them all with you, ad nauseam, on some days." Terrin slapped the blade, and it twisted around his finger like a propeller before he tossed it in the air to catch it by the hilt. "I don't think I did that because I was loyal to my duty." He finally took his eyes off the sword and pinned me with a dark look. "In fact, I can recall many times that my behavior deviated from my duty. I've made sacrifices on your behalf—and I don't mean to save your life. I mean, that my life has been on hold since I've met you. Everything I have ever done since meeting you has been in service to you. That is not just loyalty, Mallory."

I nodded, conceding that his actions were not solely obligations. "I know. I shouldn't have said that."

He approached me and stood on the other side of the doorway. "I do think that I confuse loyalty and obedience sometimes. I think that my intentions are good, but it's hard to break old habits. Sometimes I just want to control you, because it's the only way I can feel you're safe." He flipped the sword around and offered me the hilt. "Perhaps it's time that I change tactics."

I shook my head. "Oh, I don't think that's a good idea. As tame as these guys are, I've actually lost to them before." He didn't lower the sword. "No, seriously, I hit myself in the foot once, almost cut my toe off."

"I recall playing that dice game about forty times in one day."

"Ugh, fine." I took the sword and marched back toward the center of the room. "I just want it noted that I am not a fighter."

"No, of course not. You're a runner." I nearly swung the sword at Terrin's head before I noticed his smirk. He was trying to be playful, but I was still too sore to enjoy his humor. "But obviously, running doesn't always work. So perhaps you should have skills beyond fast feet."

Terrin pushed in behind me, surprising me as he pressed himself against me like a glove. He pulled my hand up, and I tried to put it where I thought he wanted it.

"Just relax," he whispered in my ear. "Let me drive for a while."

I cleared my throat. "I thought I wasn't supposed to surrender to you."

"Only if I try to stick something where it doesn't belong." I scoffed, but I went limp so he could play with me like a doll. He brought his hand to my hip and directed me to angle my body toward one of the biomechanoids. "In swordplay, the object is to create less of a target. You angle your body and then parry and thrust." He mimicked the movements I had done. "This is all well and good if you are fighting with a sword. But this is a *mnocha*."

I looked up at him and tried to say the unfamiliar word with his inflection. He said it again, slower, allowing me to see the movement of his mouth. Because Terrin learned the empire's tongue at a young age, he rarely spoke his home language. Which meant I only knew the few cusswords he had grumbled under his breath at me.

"I've never heard you call it that before."

"Because I've never used it like that before. Mnocha means 'deliverer of death.'"

"Oh."

"A short sword, though useful in a defensive situation with other swords, is meant to be used as a knife. It is not designed to fight with. It is designed to kill with. That's why it is so light." Terrin moved my body again to face the soldier. "If you were a gattaw, your goal would be to stab your opponent right through the heart." He directed my sword toward the rib cage. "But I doubt you could get the sword through the ribs. Instead, you should aim for the throat." He directed the sword to the cleft in the man's throat. "Do not hesitate, or you will only injure him."

He released me and stepped away. "Also, if you are ever in a situation with a male gattaw, you should aim for the inner thigh. Almost as if you are aiming to castrate him." Terrin reached for my hand and directed it downward to his groin. Rather than prudishly flee from the lesson, I crouched down and averted my gaze as he positioned my hand right where his thigh transitioned into his buttocks. "The human femoral artery is deep within the leg, but in the male gattaw, it skirts the surface before descending into the legs. Can you feel the pulse?"

I nodded. I felt his pulse. I also felt my own.

"It's a male gattaw's greatest weakness. It's said that this is the reason oral sex never became tolerable to female gattaw. Too dangerous to have teeth so close to our Achilles' heel."

I made an effort to laugh at his joke, but I couldn't really focus on anything beyond my proximity to his very pronounced pants bulge. When he had said nothing else, but also hadn't directed my hand away, I looked up at him.

When we locked eyes, I saw the same frozen concern that I was certain that I was wearing. While he may have been showing me his anatomy for the grander purpose, it was quickly devolving into a scene from a bad porno. We were playing a dirty game of chicken and one of us needed to flinch.

But neither of us did.

As I crouched there looking up at him like a virgin student willing to learn *anything* from her teacher—god help me—I licked my lips. His eyes immediately went to my mouth. I could see the desire in his eyes, and I was glad for it. Not because there was much to do about it, but because I wanted to know it was there. That he was just as tortured by this arrangement as I was.

I felt his pulse increasing, and I considered my options. Not the romantic happily ever after ones, but the in-the-moment, right-now options. What could I do to satisfy this endlessly irritating itch we were both experiencing?

Without regard to the outcome, the fallout, or the emotions I was toying with, I shifted my hand ever so slowly. I slipped out from beneath his fingers and moved my hand beneath the mound of flesh trapped in his suit.

He gaped at me, eyes wide with shock and desire. His mouth draped open as if he wanted to tell me to stop, but couldn't.

I tentatively stroked him, not wanting to rush the stimulation. In time, his spurs would eject and reduce my options for quick stimulation. It was a tricky task, but it was possible. Sadly, I had researched it far too many times. I had just never had the opportunity to try it.

Terrin's breathing had increased, just as mine had. My hand was shaking—fearful that I was inciting as much of his anger as I was his arousal. I kept my eyes on him, waiting for him to stop me. Waiting for him to tell me I was a bad, bad girl—Christ! This was a porno!

I continued to massage him until he was longer and harder. Then I took my seduction a step further. Surprising both him and myself, I leaned forward and licked the length hiding in his uniform.

His calmness broke and several gattaw curse words came flying out of his mouth. He grabbed me by the shoulders and lifted me off the floor. He backed me across the bay and pressed me against the frame of the doorway. He continued to speak in his native language, no doubt lecturing me. Despite his scolding tone, he didn't look as angry as I expected. He looked positively frightened.

When he realized that none of his words were sinking in, he stopped cussing and looked at the floor between us. I was still trembling—partly from adrenaline and partly from nerves. I had never gone this far. Never trespassed this deeply. "Show me how," I whispered.

"What?" He looked up.

"Teach me how to please you." I knew it was a line directly from that porno, but I was serious. I was tired of fighting with him. Tired of fighting against my desire. We may not have been biologically compatible, but imperfect passion was, at least, passion.

I watched him, watching me, panting slightly and considering my request. He wasn't storming off, so that was a good sign.

Then his expression changed into something very stern. He moved closer to me and I shrunk back a little, waiting for the chastising to begin, but he didn't say a word before he kissed me.

His lips were warm and inviting, teasing my nerve endings down to my toes. He moved from my lips to my jawline and then to my neck. My breath hitched as his mouth opened wide against my skin, but he didn't bite. He dragged his tongue across me, tasting me.

When he drew back, he locked eyes with me. There was a question there and also a warning. We both knew this was stupid, but neither one of us had the strength to stop it.

He reached down and ripped his sword from my hand. I hadn't even realized I was still holding it. He tossed it in the center of the bay, as if declaring that I could no longer defend myself against him.

Wasn't that the truth?

Terrin lifted me up, pushing me back into the wall, grinding himself against me. I gasped, my mind suddenly split between pleasure and disbelief. I couldn't believe he was doing this. I surrendered to the moment as he rocked against me, trailing his lips down my neck. I waited for reality to hit him. To draw him away from me. Instead, he carried me to my quarters and dropped me onto the bed.

"Terrin," I cautioned him, as he pushed my legs apart and crawled on top of me. I let out a little whimper as he once again moved against me, pressing his barely contained girth against my core. I cursed and pulled him toward me. "What about the spurs?" I rasped, wondering how much longer we could keep this up.

He moved his mouth to my ear, biting my earlobe. "It's puncture-proof fabric, remember?"

The reality of the situation hit me. This was happening. And I had no intention of stopping it.

I pulled Terrin forward and kissed him between my stuttered breaths. He brushed my hair back and caressed my cheek before pinching the tag of my zipper and drawing it down. I glanced down at my increasingly longer neckline.

He stopped the zipper at my belly button. His hand slid under the fabric of my jumpsuit, squeezing and caressing my breast. He shifted his mouth down to kiss my already tantalized flesh. Lost to the moment, I arched my back, demanding to get more of him. I said his name again, but it was no longer spoken so much as breathed.

He resumed a steady pressure against me, rocking our bodies together to ease months and years of pent-up desires. I moaned as the pleasure built. I grabbed his shoulders, digging my nails into the durable fabric of his suit. Terrin increased his pace to hasten my rise.

I had dreamed of the pleasure Terrin could provide, but oddly, I had never imagined this scenario. I never thought we could achieve a fervent, unplanned intimacy like this.

He gazed down at me as I panted, trying to keep control of myself, but there was no room for delay while he wielded my body. I writhed and cried out, falling over the rising summit of pleasure.

Almost before the tension in my body released, Terrin was off me and landing against the back wall of the room. I stared in shock at the biomechanoid soldier standing over me.

"What the hell?" Terrin asked as he stood back up.

I looked at the biomechanoid soldier with confusion. He must have thought that Terrin was attacking me and intervened. "I don't know. I think it's malfunctioning."

The guard raised his arm and pointed it at Terrin. "Stay the hell away from my wife," a computerized voice said.

Terrin narrowed his eyes at the soldier just as mine widened. "Rayne?" I questioned.

STOOGES

The soldier's head turned on its predetermined axis. "Kit," it answered back.

I gasped and pulled the zipper of my jumpsuit back up. I looked at Terrin, who was now approaching the biomechanoid like it was a bomb about to go off. "Rayne? Are you linked to this thing? Where are you?"

"Goddamn it, Turner," the soldier's mechanized voice said. "I said not yet! ... Like I was going to sit there and watch him rape her!"

I glanced at Terrin—and my face reddened with shame. Rayne had obviously misinterpreted my screams of pleasure as screams of distress. Terrin all but rolled his eyes. "That's not—"

"I am sick and tired of your women interfering in our operations." The robot continued to argue with himself, presumably catching both sides of an argument on one microphone. "They can hear everything you are saying, you idiots." The soldier suddenly snapped to attention and looked around the room at both of our confused faces. "It's too late, anyway. Both of you, get on a controller."

A moment later, two soldiers arrived at the door to the room. One of them offered me a hand up and I took it. "Rayne?" I questioned.

"I'm Ayil." The robot raised his hand, nearly hitting my chin as it did. "Oh, sorry, this is harder than I thought." The computerized voice said. The hand moved down as if to shake my hand.

"Is it really you?" I asked.

"Yes. Miss me?" Robo-Ayil asked. Even though it wasn't the real Ayil inside the suit, I hugged the soldier. "Hey, where did you go?"

"She's hugging you, you idiot," the other guard said—presumably Rayne.

"Oh." Ayil's soldier wrapped his arms around me for a hug.

"Too tight, too tight," I complained when my back cracked.

"Sorry, sorry." He released.

"What's going on?" Terrin drew me away from Ayil's soldier. The soldier under Rayne's control turned his head to watch us.

"It's a premature rescue," the first robot said—presumably Reynard, now. "Because someone can't understand the words, 'don't interact.'"

"Where are you?" I asked. Terrin kept his hand on my shoulder. I wasn't sure if that was for my benefit, Rayne's, or if he just needed me to stand in front of him for a little while longer.

"Not far." Rey pointed out in a seemingly random direction. "We have been following you since you left Inferno."

"You've been here the whole time?"

Rayne closed the door to the room. "We couldn't tell you."

"The biomechanoids have no memory entry of us taking them over." Rey's soldier moved around the bed to join us. "But we couldn't risk Agate seeing us corresponding with you."

"Can you get us out of here?" I asked.

"Absolutely not," Rey said.

"What?"

"He means not yet." Ayil moved forward and knocked his fist against the head of Rey's puppet.

"Not until you reach the medical base," Rey continued to explain. "I haven't been able to locate it since I helped Kessler escape. The people on board don't even know where they are."

"How long will that be?"

"Shouldn't be long now. We are starting to get traces of biological residue."

"Residue?" I asked.

"Poop, Kit," Ayil answered.

"Eew."

Rey's robot shrugged. "It's a stationary base."

"What happens when we reach the base?" Terrin retracted his hand from my shoulder and stepped out from behind me.

Ayil's soldier shifted his gaze down for a moment. "Nice outfit."

Terrin gave him a sidelong glare.

"Once we have the location of the base, I will do what I should have done after I extracted Kessler. Destroy it."

"Wait, no you can't," I insisted. "Aresties is there. She's sick."

"We know. We heard the conversation with Agate. We heard what his plans were for her. That's why I am going to destroy the base."

"No, we can save her. They have all the cures right there. We can inoculate her before we take her off."

"I'm afraid an operation of that nature would be impossible. Even if the lab wasn't already a fortress, this battlerunner is bringing thousands of soldiers with it. There is no way that we would succeed in escaping with her and the child."

"Killing Aresties kills my child, Rey."

"The decision has already been made." Although everything up to that was one emotionless response, his next words felt even colder. "The decision is unanimous."

I turned my attention to the two biomechanoids. I searched their lacking faces for the answer. "This is what you want, Rayne."

"Want? No. But you've seen the virus, Kit. You know what we are risking by letting anyone get exposed."

I tried to hear his rationale for letting Rey kill our child. I tried to understand, but the wound was still too fresh to feel anything but grief. I hadn't felt my child stirring inside of me. I hadn't felt him or her in my arms. And yet, I felt that loss like a knife to my heart.

"It's what we have to do, Kit," Ayil said. "Kessler doesn't believe she can be saved at this stage. And if she dies, the baby will die too."

"Ayil? Are you telling me to give up?"

"I..." The biomechanoid dropped as if someone had taken their hands off his strings.

"Ayil?"

Rayne stepped forward. "We aren't sure, but we suspect that Edric is on the medical base, too."

I shook my head. "Oh, no."

"Did Agate ever imply that he had collected both pods?" Terrin asked me.

"No, and I didn't think to ask. I was so preoccupied with Aresties." I moved to Ayil's soldier and pushed his head up to look at me. "Ayil, I'm so sorry. I didn't want any of this."

"There's nothing you could do to stop this, Mallory." Terrin rested his hand back on my shoulder.

"But you do have a chance to save thousands—possibly millions of lives," Rey said. "I know this sacrifice is difficult and I don't relish killing hundreds of my former friends and coworkers either, but it must be done. We all must make this choice to keep this virus contained."

"Is there no other option?" Terrin asked.

There was a long pause before Rey responded. "No. The child has to die."

Loss

I woke that night tucked into Terrin's arms. I had spent the better part of the evening crying. It was only when I was near dehydrated that I fell asleep. As miserable as I was, I was grateful to have him here with me. To keep me from doing something rash.

I shifted to look at him and found him fast asleep and breathing so slowly that I almost thought he was dead. Sometime in the night, he had kicked off my makeshift blankets and tangled himself up in the process. Apparently, our huddled bodies were too much heat, even for him.

Before this imprisonment, I had never even seen him sleep. As a child, I had convinced myself that he never slept, but he most likely rested during my school lessons.

I raised my hand to stroke his cheek, taking advantage of his unconscious state so I could explore him. Although I knew what his hands and lips felt like all too well, our short intimacies had never allowed me the time to touch him the way I wanted to.

I moved my hand down the hard sinew of his chest. I traced my finger along his raised sternum to his belly. Here his skin softened, from silk to soft leather, then to velvet. I noted the more oblong shape of his belly-button before

I reached the band of his undergarment. I could see the mound under the fabric well enough to know he was a well-endowed man.

The pleasure I'd recently experienced tempted me to reach deeper and caress his carnal muscle. But I didn't want to be with him simply to escape my pain. I also didn't want Rayne to interrupt us again. As certain as I was that my relationship with Rayne had taken its course, I also didn't want to shove my experimentation with Terrin in his face.

As I traced my fingers along the stretch fabric of Terrin's undergarment, I noticed something rough. I pushed back the fabric to inspect the dark red spots on his lower belly. He had several minor injuries that I suddenly realized were self-inflicted. The puncture proof fabric he was wearing protected me from his barbed member, but it did nothing to protect him.

Even with our best solution so far to our impediments, one of us was still getting hurt.

Thrown Bone

The next morning, I woke before Terrin and extricated myself from the bed quietly so I didn't disturb him. I slipped over to the infirmary for a quick shower—which I desperately needed to feel replenished enough to deal with what was coming.

After my hair and body were clean, I stood in the tepid water, refusing to confront reality. When a warm body pressed up against me, I jumped, even though I knew it was Terrin. I leaned against him, inviting his arms to wrap around me. I lived to be in his arms and, for the first time, I wasn't thinking about the future. All I wanted was right now.

"How are you feeling?" he whispered in my ear as he gave me a gentle squeeze.

"I'm... surviving."

"We'll get through this." He kissed my cheek and for nearly a minute, he simply held me while the recycled water pelted us. Then ever so slowly he caressed my belly with one hand while his other hand slipped over my breast, teasing the flesh tensed by the cool water.

He moved his other hand progressively lower, giving me a chance to refuse his attentions. By the time he transitioned from wet skin to whetted flesh, I was more than ready for him.

I pushed back against him as he teased me. I panted and writhed, wanting to be so much closer to him. As if trying to satisfy that desire, he dipped his fingers inside of me. Giving me at least some of what we were missing.

I shamelessly pressed into his hand, begging for more. And he gave it—diving as deeply as he could, squeezing my breasts, and kissing my neck. The world disappeared, and I welcomed the reprieve. I didn't care if I ever returned to reality.

I surrendered to my mounting arousal and muffled my moaned satisfaction against his neck, so I didn't draw the attention of the biomechanoids standing guard outside the door.

Realizing I was once again leaving Terrin on simmer, I turned to attend to him. As I reached for his erection, he intercepted my hands and kissed them. "It's alright."

"Don't you at least want to try?" I asked, but didn't wait for his answer. I pulled one hand free and grabbed his length at the base. Since his spurs were higher up, I at least had some freedom to move in a traditional manner.

Terrin closed his eyes for a moment, enjoying what I offered so far. When he gripped my shoulders, I began the milking technique I had learned from not-so-prudish sources. His eyes flapped open, apparently surprised that I didn't need as much instruction as I claimed. "Careful," he whispered.

He kept his eyes pinned on me as I proceeded with two hands, drawing only upward to keep the spurs down. It was a bit like avoiding road spikes.

As I developed a rhythm, he clutched my shoulders, then he shifted one hand to fondle my breast. When he couldn't take it anymore, he descended on my mouth. The deep kiss sent shivers down into my belly. Distracted by my desire, I lost track of my rhythm and shifted my hand back down his erection. I yelped at the sensation of grabbing a sticker patch.

Terrin pulled back to check on me. As I looked down, I saw my hand was bleeding. "Shit," I hissed, examining the tiny cuts on my hand. They were far from deep, but much like any paper cut—they hurt like hell. "Sorry." I reached down to continue my work, but Terrin retrieved my hand after a single stroke.

"No," was all he said.

"It's not that bad. I can continue."

Terrin sighed and shut the water off. He grabbed my towel and wrapped it around me. "If you really want to do this, then you are going to have to get used to disappointment."

"I know, but... What about you?"

Terrin looked me over, a certain admiration in his eyes that I only ever saw on rare occasions. "It's not about that right now... and that's okay." He dragged his finger down my cheek before giving me a rather chaste kiss on the cheek. "Go, get dressed. We need to get prepared for our arrival at the space station."

I nodded, though there wasn't much we could do to prepare. Nor did we even know when we were arriving. Rey had estimated 24 hours, but that depended highly on fecal evacuation protocols.

When I reached the door, I turned back. "Maybe later we could try the suits again."

Terrin turned back and gave me a somber smile. "Of course."

It took me until I reached my quarters to come to the very sad realization that Terrin was only humoring me. Not about the suits, but about all of it. He said this wasn't about him, and he was right. I thought he had finally succumbed to his desires, but he hadn't. He had succumbed to mine. Last night and this morning were just his ways of finally giving me what I want.

And why not? We were prisoners of the Coalition, unlikely to escape, and without a tremendous hope for survival—at least we were prior to our knowledge of Rey's Peeping Toms.

Terrin was just granting the wish of a dying woman.

Base

I had barely gotten dressed before an alert sounded throughout the ship and the biomechanoids came to life—so to speak—doing routine procedures. Given the circumstances, I could only assume that they were preparing to dock with the space station.

"Already?" Terrin asked as he entered my quarters, wet from his shower.

"I guess so." I slipped into a new suit while Terrin dried off a bit. I headed out the door, but he grabbed my arm.

"Wait for me."

I was more than a little annoyed, but I understood his concerns. There were no assurances that our arrival at the base had to be with hearts still beating. If the biomechanoids turned on us, we would have no hope of survival, but that didn't mean Terrin wouldn't want to try.

I waited impatiently as he slipped into his suit. He grabbed his short sword and tossed it to me. Together, we headed out to the main bay and approached the mammoth viewscreen, searching for our destination. After a few minutes, a dot appeared in the distance—growing bigger by the second.

Unlike a traditional ship, designed for speed and maneuverability, the Coalition designed the medical base for energy efficiency and real estate. The entire structure was the size of eight city blocks and five stories high. But it didn't look like a city to me so much as an island.

A frightening island of Dr. Moreau, that was likely to contain monsters... just like me.

In the center of the base was a massive antenna for long-range communication. On the outer edges were thousands of vapor traps and friction generators that ensured the ship had all the necessities for life. Give or take a few yearly deliveries of food and lab supplies. No one was likely to visit this place very often.

Terrin reached over and took my hand, linking his fingers in mine. Despite our recent interactions, the contact felt strange. It was a different type of intimacy. Something we hadn't shared before. I gripped his hand and waited for Rey to arrive, bringing the attack that would bring about the end of a war, as well as the death of my friend, my child, and adoptive nephew. It was ironic that I had only just saved them from this fate on my ship. Perhaps there really was such a thing as destiny. It wasn't just a finish line as I had presumed, but a net that closed in around you long before you knew it trapped you.

"I'm proud of you, Mallory," Terrin said.

"For what?" I asked, wiping away a tear with my other hand.

"I know this isn't the path you would have chosen, but I am glad you've accepted it."

Terrin had said little about Rey's plan, beyond consoling me. I presumed he felt like his input didn't matter, since he was the only one not losing a loved one with this plan. "I'm not sure I was given a choice, but I've only just begun to understand the lengths that Agate will go to destroy the empire. If this is the only chance we have to destroy his operation, then so be it. I just hate that I can't save them."

"We all do." He squeezed my hand and nodded out toward the base. "If it's any consolation, I believe that Aresties would gladly sacrifice herself to protect the crown." I scoffed, a little surprised by the way he had phrased her devotion. I was certain that Aresties would do anything to protect Ayil and myself, just as we would her, but I hadn't really thought of her as being political. However, the Coalition's inhumane tactics had helped sway many people to share the hope of unity that the empire provided. "Here they come."

I saw Rey's ship coming into view on the far edge of the view window. They were coming up fast, passing the battlerunner with ease. Despite seeing the ship with my own eyes, the battlerunner's sensors did not bleat, and the alarms did not sound. The ship and its soldiers were blind to the attack about to take place.

The torpedo tubes lit on the side of Rey's ship, sending four missiles toward the base. Compared to land attacks, these projectiles glided through space as if in slow motion. Motility was never an issue for them, just directionality, which was already programmed in. Short of destruction, the missiles would hit four vital parts of the ship. A chain reaction would mean instant death for nearly half the crew. The rest would die from lack of life support.

The remaining carcass of the base would be what the Coalition, not-so-lovingly, referred to as "sunken treasure." They would salvage what they could from the ship and retrieve the bodies of the dead for their army. However, since it was the Coalition being killed this time,

I had to wonder if they would still be so callous with their own.

Sensing the approaching projectiles, the defensive systems activated on the base and cannons deployed to shoot them down. The pulse blasts ricocheted off the torpedoes' built-in shields, preventing them from prematurely detonating.

The defense systems in the battlerunner activated shortly after. I jumped to the first lit panel and tried manually deactivating the alarm, but the ship's design prioritized a computer interface over human interaction.

A short, sharp droning sound bellowed across the ship and the already dim lighting went down to near darkness. The remaining at-ease soldiers that lined the bay simultaneously stomped into alert poses. All heads turned in our direction, followed by a twist of the bodies. A single, slightly out of sync step brought the entire army one step closer to us.

Terrin yanked me behind him as the second step clapped thunder through the bay. The third came quicker, echoing through the chamber. The fourth and fifth steps brought the first line just a few feet away from us.

Terrin tensed, ready, if not able, to fight the entire army off. Before anyone could throw any punches, the first line turned and marched toward the outer walls. The line behind them stepped forward in their place and also turned. Like ants on a mission, they filed to the edges of the bay and ascended the adjacent stairwells in the bays—allowing them access to the upper decks. Allowing them access to the jetships.

I breathed a sigh of relief for our own safety, only to remember that Rey was about to get some company.

I whipped back to look at the viewscreen. I just glimpsed the torpedoes' final approach. Consecutively, they disappeared into the ship. One, two, three, four.

Tears sprung to my eyes, and I waited for the base to exhale its last four breaths in a puff of fire. Soon after, the shrapnel would shoot forth like glitter, interspersed with the bodies of our victims.

But nothing happened.

I looked at Terrin. "What just happened?"

He shook his head, also perplexed. "I'm not sure. They went in, but—there." He pointed to the bottom of the base where the torpedoes were coming out fully intact. They floated away, still proceeding on their path, not knowing that they hadn't hit what Rey had intended them to. But perhaps they had hit exactly what the Coalition wanted them to.

"Oh my, God." I leaned forward as if that might improve my view. I pointed out the flicker in the far corner, as if the screen was on the fritz, but it wasn't the screen. It was the base. "The base is part hologram." I turned to Terrin. "Rey just targeted absolutely nothing."

I could only imagine what Rey was thinking at this moment. If he wasn't banging on his controls and frothing with anger, he was about to.

The battlerunner vibrated, and the jetships sprang forth like a swarm appearing on the screen as sleek black missiles aimed directly at Rey's ship. They began firing, just as Rey did. The sparks of energy bounced and dissipated off the shields of the jetships. Rey's ship, however, absorbed the onslaught across his hull using a network of powerful capacitors.

"Why are we still heading to base?" Terrin pointed out to the base that was getting steadily closer, despite the obvious inconvenience of a death match happening just outside. A port opened, ready to receive the battlerunner's docking ring. "We do not want to be on that base when Rey is finished with those jetships." Terrin looked at me with genuine concern.

"I'm not sure we have a choice," I mumbled.

Before the base could eclipse my view of Rey's ship, I watched the hull bloom with a yellow bubble of energy, just like the Starla used to fend off her attackers. The energy dispersed in a spherical wave, decimating the shields of the attacking ships. It was truly magnificent. Even the battlerunner was not immune to the shield-dissolving effects.

I was proud and full of hope for a quick rescue. Reynard really was a talented magician of warfare, and he deserved almost all the clout his triplicated presence received. However, my mental applause quickly died away as I watched one of the remaining jetships dive directly into his hull, kamikaze style.

"Oh!" I covered my mouth as the nose penetrated the ship, damaging god knows what—or who. "Terrin!" I whined, though I knew there was nothing he could do to help them either. I pounded on the controls as the ship disappeared over the horizon of the base. The last I saw of Rey's ship, it was using a mass artillery defense, shooting at multiple jetships at once. Without shields, they were just buzzing flies to him. Unfortunately, like flies, the sheer number of them ensured a few were bound to reach their targets.

That was the true power of a biomechanoid army. A dead army had nothing to live for, so self-sacrifice was always an option. Loyal, lethal, and replaceable. Just what a dictator needs in his soldiers.

"They aren't going to help us anytime soon. Can you at least override the doors so we aren't connected to their life support?" Terrin asked.

"I can't do anything with this thing." I looked at the port looming just ahead of us. We were landing on the base whether or not we wanted to. Terrin was right that we didn't want to be on it during this battle. It was only a matter of time before Rey hit something vital enough to destroy it. And regardless of who was on the base, he was not likely to stop his attack.

Despite all of that, I turned to Terrin and with determination settling into my backbone, I said, "I'm going to save my child."

Into the Lion's Mouth

Terrin hadn't argued with me. He was either aware of how much danger we were already in, regardless of my heroics, or he simply knew he couldn't persuade me otherwise.

Once the ships coupled, Terrin and I stepped off the battlerunner and onto the medical base. The halls were glowing intermittently with red, warning the staff that shit was about to hit the fan. Little did any of them know, it had hit the fan the minute I was born. I was quickly becoming a plague on the people that had designed me, and a part of me enjoyed that. It was the pride of turning on the ones that had tried to destroy my entire life.

Two men in lab coats ran past us, only giving Terrin a second glance as they scurried to their destination somewhere around the bend. Since no one appeared to be interested in detaining us, we moved to a welcome panel on the wall. I pressed 'start' and a tall, unnaturally skinny woman appeared on the screen. "Welcome to The Island. How may I direct you?" she asked.

I snorted at the accuracy. "Where's the infirmary?" I asked.

"The infirmary is at the center of the station on decks two, three, and four," the computer responded and gave me a map to the nearest entry point. She was surprisingly helpful, but I was certain that most of the people in here were supposed to be here. I headed that way just as an impact hit the station.

The previously quiet security system added blaring alarms to the blinking red lights. Vibrations traveled throughout the base, and for a moment my feet froze to the floor. A useless safety protocol, no doubt designed to keep people from flying out into space in the event of decompression.

Once the gravity subsided, we ran down the gently curving hall toward the infirmary. Another impact hit the base, and an awful creak echoed through the halls. The alarms shut off and so did the lights—all the lights. I cussed in complete darkness and listened to the sounds of screeching metal and people screaming.

"I can't see anything." I flailed my arms, fearing that unrealistic things were in my path.

"This way." Terrin stepped ahead of me and took me by the hand. I jogged forward with him, but I lagged when I realized we were going toward the sounds of the screams.

"Terrin," I whispered his name and squeezed his hand.

"There's some debris up ahead," he said. "We'll need to slow down. Stay close to me."

"Okay."

He guided us forward, through the smell of smoke and toward the screaming. I stumbled over a piece of wreckage and took hold of Terrin's arm for more support. The second piece I stepped on made me unsteady and I questioned what I was feeling. The third piece of "wreckage" made a squelching sound under my foot and put my heart into a heavy thumping beat. "Terrin," I whimpered more than spoke.

"Just keep going, Mallory. It's just ahead."

I ignored my concerns and kept stepping across the sea of unsteady, malleable debris that was on the floor of the hall. I tried not to think about how it had gotten there or why there was so much of it. All I knew was that, at that moment, I was happy to have human eyes.

Unfortunately, I still had human ears. The screaming woman who made me want to turn tail and run for my life was right next to me as we maneuvered through the dark. Something slapped against my ankle and I gasped. Then a hand gripped onto my calf, nails digging into the protective black cloth. The screaming stopped and the voice just below me rasped. "Help me! Please!"

"Keep moving, Mallory." Terrin tugged me forward, and I tried to take a step. "We can't help her."

The woman clamped onto me and nearly tripped me. "Please!" she screamed, no longer begging, but demanding that I save her. "Please!" she continued to screech.

"Terrin," I said again, unsure if I could extricate myself from her grip. He turned to face me and I could feel his breath on my face. I tried to look into his eyes, or as near to them as I remembered them to be. I felt the blade on my hip shift and I reached to grab it, but realized that Terrin was the one moving it.

His lips touched mine, and I jumped again, before receiving the oddly timed kiss. His body jolted against me and the screaming pleas for help stopped. The hand gripping my calf released and dropped to the floor. Terrin surrendered my lips and holstered his blade back on my hip.

He pulled me forward urgently for another few feet and then we stopped. "Eyes forward," he commanded just as a light filled the hall from an opening door. We stepped into the junction and, as requested, I did not look behind us. I didn't want to know what had happened to the people behind us. The less I knew about my options for demise, the better. I was already familiar with several paths to death. I didn't need another.

As soon as the door closed behind us, the door before us opened. We ran down the brightly lit white hall. The upper portion of the rounded passageway had inset windows offering us a view of the battle happening outside. I was pleased that Rey's ship was still intact—albeit penetrated by several jetships.

Unfortunately, the shrapnel the battle was creating was impacting the base. More than a few jetships, blown off their course, had buried into its surface. One of which was no doubt behind us.

In addition, two torpedoes were barreling across the vacuum of space in search of anything worth hitting. The off-the-cuff shots weren't likely to destroy the station as Rey wanted, but they would certainly kill its occupants, one section at a time. And since the list of occupants included us, I hesitated to celebrate his victory in this battle.

The torpedoes hit the base, close to our section. "Faster!" Terrin yelled, increasing his already fast pace to an Olympic level. I had very little to offer beyond lengthening my strides. It felt like progress, but I was still just a human and naturally fell behind him.

I could see from the corner of my eye the impact blooming outside. The burst of fire quickly died, followed by an expulsion of rubble. What size of debris, and how much, was the biggest concern in situations such as these. Especially since our walkway was right in the shrapnel's path.

"Mallory!" Terrin yelled from the security of the junction section. All he had to do was shut the door and he would be safe, but I knew from the look on his face that he wouldn't. He was already latching himself onto the door handle, prepared for the inevitable decompression. He reached out his hand as if I merely needed to reach him to survive. However, the expanse of six more feet wouldn't cut it.

A loud bleat filled the hall just as the crinkling and snapping of heavy plastic warned me of the base's fractured hull. My feet froze beneath me and I fell forward. Terrin's wide eyes stared back at me, just a few footsteps away from me.

The fear of losing my life was not unfamiliar to me, and yet each time was like a new nerve-racking experience. I was tired of being at death's door. My more recent close calls were leaving a sour taste in my brain that I feared would affect my sanity.

"Mallory, look!" Terrin pointed behind me, his face in awe of what he was looking at.

My boots released, and I rolled over. Had I been upright, I would have dropped to the floor, anyway. The massive spiked sculpture of amber behind me was frighteningly beautiful. The extensive protective matrix that was embedded into the hull had activated as the debris tore through the walkway. Threads of golden orange reached out to me and into space, creating a frozen explosion that had ultimately saved me from another round of Russian roulette with the universe's deadly embrace.

Grateful to still have my life, I jumped up and ran to the next junction to join Terrin. As one door closed, another opened, and we both tumbled down the next walkway in the grip of an aberrant false gravity.

Slide

"We don't have time for this!" Terrin yelled at me as I rolled past him again. I had been tumbling back and forth down the same walkway for the past few minutes. The gravity disruption had left both halves of the hall in steep opposing gradients. Rolling down the walkway to one end and then back again bumped and bruised me everywhere. I didn't have the height necessary to brace myself in the middle, as Terrin had. He was making his way slowly to the other end, but I could see this method of tension climbing was taking him a great deal of effort.

"I have an idea!" I called back to him. "Can you keep yourself braced?"

"Yes!"

"Okay, here I come!" I hollered as I tumbled back down to him. I had been trying to avoid hitting him before, but now I aimed right at him.

I hit him, forcing an "*uff*" from him. "Sorry," I whispered as I realized I had nearly landed against his crotch.

"It's alright. Just warn me next time you want to play so rough."

I chuckled as I positioned myself in front of him, or from gravity's perspective, on top of him. He kept his eyes on me as I awkwardly dragged myself over him, placing myself in a rather familiar position.

"You are intending to save me, right, Mallory? Or did you just want to get one more tryst in before you die?"

"Oh, sorry, I was actually just going to save you."

"Mmm, disappointing, I guess I'll just have to figure out a way to express my gratitude later."

I laughed nervously. "Terrin, you shouldn't distract me while we are in life-and-death situations."

"Good point. Why don't you tell me what you are going to do?"

"Um, well, the plan is for me to get on your back and then we will brace against each other as we walk down the tube together." Terrin's face shifted into worry, but he nodded. "Okay, this first part is all me, so don't let go. If I drop, I'll start over."

"That sounds good, but I do want to point out that Rey just dropped two more torpedoes on the far end of the base."

I looked up out through the windows and saw an enormous piece of the base breaking away from itself. It wasn't a danger to us since it was floating laterally, but nearly a quarter of the base was now disconnected. That meant the structure would start quarantining necessary sections to preserve its most valuable data and projects. Aresties would be inaccessible to us soon.

"So, I'm hurrying." After a few seconds of calculating my downward fall, I made a move I was certain I couldn't replicate, even on my best day. Bracing my foot against his ankle and grabbing tight onto his biceps, I slipped the other half of my body between him and my connections. I flopped out underneath him, dragged down by the gravity that, if I was not mistaken, was increasing.

Terrin grunted and his biceps went taut. I swung my free-hanging foot up to latch onto his other ankle and grabbed his other arm to balance my weight. I hung there a moment again, positioned as his human backpack, to consider the best method for us to get ourselves juxtaposed. Unfortunately, there was only one way to do it. We had to drop.

"Ready when you are," Terrin said, already making the same prediction.

"On three?"

"On three," he agreed.

I counted down as evenly as I could to three, and Terrin released his bracing arms and legs. We dropped nearly to the door before our boots skidded to a stop on the interior walls of the corridor. Despite the imbalance of our weight and height, we had achieved the proper tension to prevent further movement.

Stretching our collaborative skills further, we took small singular steps, inching our way down to—or up to the door. Terrin breathed a sigh of relief as he pushed the button to open the door to what should have been the safe interior of the ship. The moment the doors opened, a gale-force wind whisked us inside.

Zombies

The alarms in the ship's interior blared. Flickering red lights created a dizzying strobe effect. Every terminal we were dragged past had an image of our friendly hostess saying, "Evacuation is mandatory."

"Hang on!" Terrin yelled, but I had no intention of giving up the safety of being his backpack.

He snagged an emergency ladder on the way by and we jerked to a stop. I nearly fell off him, but regained enough grip to stay with him as he climbed up—or possibly down the access shaft. Once we were clear of the section with the mandatory evacuation procedure, we reoriented ourselves to proper gravity.

Or to put it another way, we fell.

"I hate gravity," I groaned after we had collided with the floor.

"Attention, medical staff," the computerized hostess popped up on every screen in the medical facility we had just dropped into. "Please depos—pos—pos—" The screens glitched a moment before proceeding. "Please deposit all specimens and samples into retrieval cartridges prior to abandoning ship. Preservation of data is your priority."

I laughed as I looked around the empty lab. I was pretty sure the downed flasks, broken test tubes, and scattered petri dishes were evidence that the data had not been the staff's priority. That, at least, left me some hope of finding Aresties. No one was likely to take the time to pack her up before they left. I just had to find her and get her into a med pod. Then Terrin and I could escape like the rest of the scientists.

Terrin approached one screen. "Computer, how much of the base is damaged?"

The images glitched again, and all the screens answered Terrin. "All four sections have damage. Life support has failed in three quarters of the ship. Evacuation is mandatory. Be advised self-destruct protocols have been activated." Terrin and I exchanged a fearful look, but we knew already that we had limited time. "The central infirmary will maintain power for thirty-two minutes. In the event of premature de—de—de—" The image glitched again. "—decompression—"

"Computer," I interrupted before the hostess could explain the near uselessness of emergency masks. "I have a deadly virus and I'm contagious," I said.

"I'm sorry to hear that," she said with cheerful sympathy. "Please report down one level to quarantine. Don't forget to cover your mouth when you cough or sneeze." She grinned, showing off her cartoonish white teeth.

"She's surprisingly helpful to enemies of the government," Terrin grumbled as we headed back to the ladder.

"Yeah, really."

Terrin grabbed the sides of the ladder and slid down to the next level gracefully. I did the same, albeit not so gracefully. "Oh, god," I jumped off the ladder, pressing my hand to my mouth and nose. "What is that smell?"

"Death," Terrin answered, surveying the room of dead bodies lying in pools of blood. Apparently, they had not been given a chance to evacuate. "Watch out." Terrin nodded behind me.

I turned around and withheld a scream for the ghoulish looking man hanging off a long rod that he had been gored by. Apart from several questions I had about how he had gotten up there, I was also curious about the pustules on his face and hands. I glanced at the people lying on the floor. They too had the blisters of disease. "Terrin."

"I see it," he answered, already on the same thought train as me.

"I don't understand what's happened here."

"I don't think we want to know," Terrin mumbled as he explored deeper into the lab, checking the labels on test tubes as he passed by several workstations.

"I didn't think this through," I said, scanning the carnage in the room that had nothing to do with Rey's attack. "This place is full of imagined plagues. What if we get infected by something?"

"If I didn't get sick from being alone in a space taxi with you for a week after your activation, I doubt Aresties will have anything that can harm me," Terrin insisted. "And there's certainly nothing here that can kill you," he added, glancing back at me.

He had certainly meant it to be a compliment, and I hoped more than believed it to be true. But this was not the environment of a controlled experimentation with gene technology. This was ground zero for a zombie apocalypse.

Even as the thought entered my mind, I sensed movement out of the corner of my eye. I turned and saw a man emerge from behind one of the lab station counters. Blood and pustules covered his face. His jaundiced, feral eyes looked directly at me. He bellowed a groaning roar before vaulting over the table to get to me.

"You were saying," I yelled to Terrin even as I back peddled away from the charging man.

"Use the sword!" Terrin instructed as he ran back across the lab to help me.

I reached for the short sword, but he was too close to defend myself. Ducking from his slashing hands, I ran only to trip over a mop a few steps later. I landed on the sword, once again unable to pull it free before the creature got to me. I reached for the mop handle, but he was already on top of me. His slobbering, bloody mouth roared, and then he descended.

Seconds away from an awful death, his head exploded. His skull shattered into unrecognizable fragments. Brain matter splattered everywhere, including in my mouth. I quickly spit out whatever had touched my tongue just as Terrin had arrived. He looked at the damage with confusion, and I realized he wasn't holding a weapon. He had not been the one to save me.

We both looked at the hallway leading to the quarantined rooms and I saw a woman standing barefoot in a blue hospital gown. Her beautiful, bulbous belly conflicted with the blood covering her body. There were purple bags under her eyes and sweat had matted her hair to her. The fact that she had the largest projectile weapon

I had ever seen in my life strapped to her shoulder did nothing to lessen her angelic image in my eyes.

"Aresties," I breathed the word as a long-awaited exhale.

Angel

I shifted to get up and my attacker, sans head, flopped forward, adding a fresh dose of blood to my face and neck. "Oh, no! Eew, help!" I gagged as Terrin pulled the body off me. I jumped to my feet. "Aresties, thank god we found you! Or you found us. Is Edric here?"

Aresties shot me an annoyed glance. "You don't have him?" Her ire dimmed. "If he's here, I haven't seen him."

I didn't like the sound of that, but with so much of the base losing power, I didn't have the luxury of extending our rescue mission to look for him. "We need to get the hell out of here. This place is gonna go belly up in less than thirty minutes."

"I know, I'm the one that did it," she said blithely and waddled over to the nearest functional computer terminal.

"Wait, what do you mean you did it?" I followed her to the terminal and watched her fingers blur as she furiously typed on the phantom keyboard. My mouth gaped as I watched the monitor flip through page after page of base code before images of the laboratory layered onto the screen. Blue prints, followed by weaponry schematics, and finally chemical formulas, popped onto the screen.

"There you are," Aresties murmured to herself.

I looked at Terrin for confirmation that this was not a familiar talent for the Aresties that I knew.

"Attention medical staff. The self-destruct protocol has been activated. Abort options have now lapsed. Deconstruction procedures have begun."

I jumped as a metal door slammed down, blocking our path back to the emergency ladder. In the distance, I heard several more thumps, indicating that someone had closed all other entry points to this section. Our list of escape options had just gotten shorter.

I gravitated to one of the hostess screens on the wall and saw the sections of the base around the central infirmary blinking yellow, except one that was already grayed out—presumably the section I had seen floating off into space. The remaining yellow pieces turned red.

The screen switched over to camera views of the four ancillary sections. One by one, the sections disintegrated, broken apart by a series of incendiary devices built into the hull. Fragments spun out, impacting and damaging two of the cameras before the screen returned to the schematic. With the surrounding base all gray, the center of the base blinked yellow. A large digital readout on the base of the image showed the number 10, followed quickly by 9:59... 9:58... 9:57.

"Ten minutes!" I flung myself back to Aresties. "Honey, we gotta go! This place is gonna blow!"

"Not just yet," she said calmly, and pulled something from her pocket to stick into the computer terminal.

I looked at Terrin, baffled and shocked that the countdown to death was not enough to motivate her to skip the hacking.

"Mallory is correct, Aresties. Our time is limited."

"I am well aware of our time constraints, but I need to finish this," she said flatly. She didn't even sound like herself. Her voice was no doubt strained from being on a respirator, but it wasn't just the dry tone that was surprising me.

"Aresties, please," I whispered, hoping that I could petition for her cooperation.

She turned to look at me, the very picture of death, and smiled. "Oh, I like your hair like that."

I instinctively touched my messy bun, which had been fashioned purely for convenience. I was certain it was not the trendy style she was thinking it was. "I... It..." I stuttered.

A loud bang sounded above us. Followed by three more.

"What's that?" I asked, ducking from the ceiling in case it was going to collapse on us.

"Probably about a half dozen ultra-bios breaking in from the floor above," Aresties said. "They don't like it when people breach the system."

A deep rumbling hum drew my attention back to the ceiling. "What are ultra-bios?" I asked.

"Bigger, better, stronger," she murmured as she stared at the download being performed on the screen.

"Perhaps we should be moving along." Terrin delicately suggested even as he placed a hand on her back.

Aresties looked up at the humming noise and then at her screen. The green line reached the end of its measure and announced in cheerful letters: download complete. She yanked the drive from the terminal and followed Terrin. After only a few steps, she winced and hissed, holding her belly.

"Are you alright?" I asked.

"No, Kit, I'm dying." I blinked at her, not sure how to react to the evaporation of my hope. "Well, help me," she barked at Terrin and he rushed forward, giving her his assistance.

Together, we moved into one of the quarantine hallways. "How are you even standing?" I asked.

"A heavy dose of painkillers and adrenaline."

"Is that safe?" I asked.

"No, but it was necessary."

A blast and crash signaled the drop of the ceiling. I listened to the consecutive thumps of six soldiers arriving at our level.

"Hurry, the med pods are just up ahead." I increased speed even though I could see that every step was anguish for Aresties.

Behind us, heavy clanking feet were coming down the hallway. I turned back. Through a cloud of dust, I saw the definition of ultra-bios as Aresties had explained them.

Hissing pistons powered the heavy thumping feet. The body—such as it was—contained armor plating instead of the vinyl puncture resistant fabric that Terrin and I were wearing. Unlike the original biomechanoids, these heads lacked shielding. A black mask covered the mouth and nose, while mechanical implants supplied them with vision. Three sets of glowing red eyes tracked us down the darkened hallway.

"Run," I screamed as the bios raised their *arms* at us. Two large cannons for each of them. A rotating barrel for projectiles on one side and on the other a wide-open tube for... missiles?

We had only just turned when a tiny white rocket breezed past my ear. It hit the floor right in front of us and exploded. We all fell back, slamming into the vibrating floor.

I heard Aresties groaning over the ringing in my ears. I coughed on dust and reached out for her. Instead, I found a hole. I looked over and saw that I was inches from falling down to the next level—and the next—and... I couldn't see past three stories down, but I was certain the fall would kill me and that was all I needed to know.

A hand grabbed me and yanked me back. I caught sight of the ultras standing guard at the end of the hall, but they didn't continue to fire. Terrin dragged me into the nearest room, which turned out to be a medical supply closet. "Why aren't they killing us?" I mumbled when I reached Aresties. She slumped against a shelf, breathing Lamaze style.

"Because they know we are already dead." Aresties pointed to the hostess screen tucked in the corner, nearly obscured by a metal shelf. The time clock read just over six minutes.

I looked at Terrin and he at me. He reached for me, and me, him. He pulled me up into an embrace. One which I had not intended to leave for the rest of my life. At least the last six minutes of it.

"What are you two doing?" Aresties snapped. "Move!"

Terrin looked over at her and immediately swung us both clear of the massive gun that Aresties had used to kill my zombie attacker. She aimed it at the interior wall of the closet and pulled the trigger. The wall exploded, leaving a rather significant hole in the plastic like material. She shot twice more, making the hole even bigger.

"Terrin, get the space suit out of that med pod," Aresties commanded.

I popped my head over to look at what she meant and saw the interior of a med pod just on the other side of the wall. Med pods lined the hall outside, but we accessed this one through the adjacent wall. I glanced at the clock, thinking there was still a chance we could survive. However, we only had access to this one pod, and our time was quickly counting down.

"Kit, put that suit on," Aresties said as she wrapped a thick white belt around her waist, positioning it under her pregnant belly. "Kit now!" she yelled.

Startled by her forceful tone, I pushed my feet into the gray jumpsuit and zipped myself in, keeping the helmet at the ready.

Aresties moved to the wall and reached through the hole. The pod activated and the glass enclosure slid open. "Terrin, get in."

Terrin looked at me. "Aresties, you must take the pod. You're carrying the child."

"Not for long, get in."

"What?" I asked.

"Get in! We are running out of time!"

Terrin glanced at me again. "What about you and Kit?" He looked back at the countdown. Only three minutes.

Aresties' face went stony, and she pulled the collar of her hospital gown down, revealing a tattoo on her chest that I recognized as a loyalist tattoo. "By the order of the queen, I command you to get into that pod right now."

Terrin's shock was there and gone, before his duty to the queen set into his bones. He moved forward, ducking through the hole and crawling into the pod. With him in place, there was no room for me or Aresties to join him.

Aresties noticed the short sword on my hip and yanked it free. She tossed it into the pod with Terrin. He peeked back out at me, wearing the same fear I was. We had less than two minutes left, and I was panicking. If I wouldn't survive this day, I at least wanted to kiss Terrin goodbye.

A *ting* sounded from the belt on Aresties' waist and a green light appeared. "What's that?" I asked.

Aresties pushed the button on the belt, and it made a noise. She winced and groaned, bracing herself against the wall. The room filled with the smell of burned hair. I gasped when I saw her lift the belt, releasing blood and fluid from her belly.

"Aresties, what are you—oh, holy fuck!" I dropped to the floor as she completed a self-induced C-section by pulling my child from the incision her belt device had created. "What are you doing?" I yelled and gathered towels for the baby.

Somewhere between reaching for the towels and bending down to help her, Aresties snipped and cauterized the umbilical cord. She reached through the hole and tucked the baby into Terrin's arms.

Aresties retracted and pushed the button to close the pod. The glass slid into place, and the machine sounded an elongated warning beep. I barely glimpsed Terrin's worried expression as he pressed his hand against the glass and mouthed my name. Then the pod disappeared, dragged out into space, leaving only a gust of stale air in its wake.

Aresties pulled my helmet from me and shoved it forcefully over my head. She pulled the girdle fabric out of the collar of my suit and attached it to the helmet, making it airtight. I could see why she had insisted that Terrin go into the tube. His horns would not fit in these helmets.

"Get in the chamber, Kit," Aresties rasped. I reluctantly stepped through the hole and placed myself in the empty chamber.

"What about... you?" When I looked back at her, I saw blood dripping from her eyes and nose. "Aresties, I'm so sorry. I didn't mean to do this to you." I shook my head, tears spilling from my eyes.

"You didn't. The Coalition did." Aresties reached into her ample bosom and pulled out the thumb drive she had used to save the data off the base's computer. She tucked the drive into one of the suit pockets and secured the snap. "Get that to your mother as soon as possible."

"Aresties, who are you?"

She pulled the massive gun off her shoulder and handed it to me. "I'm your friend, Kit. I have always been your friend." She pushed a few buttons on the exit shaft, no doubt setting it to an emergency purge setting. She looked back at me and smiled. A profound sadness replaced the warmth I usually felt when confronted by her cheerful disposition. "Congratulations," she whispered. "It's a girl."

I broke into tears, sucking in a stuttered breath. The exterior hatch opened and before I could say goodbye or thank her, the vacuum of space dragged away.

I whipped past layers and layers of metal like a water slide. Screaming my anguish into my helmet, I knew, once and for all, I had lost my friend. And it was all because of the Coalition.

I erupted into the icy embrace of space, but I felt anything but cold. The heat of my anger made me want to rip apart every biomechanoid I could find, and destroy every jetship I could reach.

Out of pure rage, I shot at the nearest ship I could see—missing it entirely. I spun around and nearly hit a piece of the floating base. My suit compensated, releasing tiny bursts of air that stabilized my movement just in time to witness the bright flash of the base's self-destruct sequence.

Light expanded out into the far reaches of the solar system like a star being born. For a moment, I could feel warmth. Then that heat pushed against me, pressing me back from an invisible collision of energy.

When the light died back down, I looked at the station and saw... nothing. The massive craft was a blur of fragments, spreading outward into space. Disseminating into trash that would eventually be a falling star to wish upon.

There was nothing left of what Kessler had created. All the research and samples, everything was gone. Except the data Aresties had retrieved for my mother. I touched the pocket she had placed the drive into. At that moment, all thoughts and plans for my life ceased to exist. The boiling rage I felt for the Coalition subsided, replaced by the cool caress of revenge. I knew what I needed to do now.

I was done running.

I was done being hunted.

It was time that I turned the tides against my enemies.

It was time to go home.

FELICIA JEDLICKA

Destiny Restored

BOOK 4 IN THE DESTINY SERIES

Destiny Restored

FELICIA JEDLICKA

Book 4

Kit has spent most of her adult life running from her responsibilities. Preordained as the next empiric queen, she had no talent for politics and no appetite for power. The expectations of the prophecy had become a weight she couldn't bear. Her only option had been to flee from her obligations and her family. But now, amid the chaos created by the Coalition's evil schemes, Kit must do the unthinkable.

She must go home.

Recruiting her mother's help to deal with the Coalition is easier said than done. Despite the obvious atrocities committed by the rebel nation, Queen Mallory's diplomatic priorities prevent her from taking military action.

With her father and sister caught in the crossfire of this cold war, Kit won't accept negotiation as an alternative to aggression. When an opportunity arises to disrupt the Coalition's strategy and retrieve Elizandra, Kit risks her life to save her sister. Unprepared for the upheaval her rebellion causes, she must expose the truth about herself to diffuse the outrage of two regimes. Even if that means putting an even bigger target on her back.

Thank you so much for reading. I hope you enjoyed the ride and if you aren't getting off here, I encourage you to sign up for my newsletter so I can return your generosity with new release updates and special offers.

Sign-Up

You can also find me on Facebook or visit my website. Keep reading!

Website

Facebook

About the Author

As a Nebraska native, and a small-town girl at that, I have very little to occupy my time beyond imagining a world outside of my own reality. By the grace of God and the seat of my pants, I have kept my waning attention span on the task of becoming an author.

So here I am, an indie author, peddling my words in cyberspace and enduring my comeuppances with an unwavering determination. I may not be a professional, and I certainly am not perfect, but if you've made it this far, you have to admit, this smartass yokel does spin quite a yarn.

From the self-inflicted sweatshop conditions of my unairconditioned childhood home, to the arthritis reaping positions of a sedentary lifestyle, I bring to you: my sarcasm, my oddity, and my heart. Take it with a grain of salt or a teaspoon of sugar, but take it for what it is: a story born of the mind, translated to paper, and gifted to you.

I thank you for your readership and even more for your support. Please recommend this book to your friends and family via any social media that you use. Word of mouth is still the best advertising and is greatly appreciated.

Most importantly, keep reading. I'll keep writing.